The Deceptions

Saloni Hazela

Invincible Publishers

First published in India in 2018 by Invincible Publishers

ISBN: 978-93-87328-51-8

Invincible Publishers
G - 120, Sushant Lok III, Sector 57, Gurgaon-122002

Opposite Kasturba Ashram, Radaur Distt Yamuna Nagar, Haryana- 135133

Acknowledgement

I would like to thank my Nanu, Baba and my father, Shailesh Hazela, for their constant support and helpful reviews. Thanks to my mom, Shailley Hazela, whose love and belief in me is deeply appreciated. A lot of love to my entire family, who have always encouraged me.

My utmost gratitude to my teachers at Costello Elementary School, Michigan, who first introduced the wonderful world of books to me and urged me to hone my writing skills.

Along with that, thanks to all my English teachers at Delhi Public School, who willingly read all my poems and stories and guided me. A sincere token of gratitude to the Principal of DPS as well, who inspired me to write my first novella.

Last, but not the least, my heartfelt gratitude to the writers of the books sitting on my bookshelves, whose stories motivated me to write my own.

Needs and wants are poles apart

1

Everything seems different at night, doesn't it? As if the drab boring place you noticed in the day did not really turn into a beautiful, midnight wonderland.

Unfortunately, no one had any idea about the horrific secrets that the night was hiding, except for me. I just stood there, staring at what I had done. I shut my eyes. The whole function-cum-party disappeared and something else, something I didn't want to see, somehow crept into my mind. Valiantly, I allowed the memories to flood my mind one last time…

~

"Trrrrring!"

I opened my eyes and stayed awake in bed for few moments, unblinking, allowing all the laziness to wash away. I sat up and placidly placed a hand on my alarm clock, smiling.

I am not one of those who groan and moan when it is time to wake up in the morning. I love mornings and soon found myself settled down with a cup of tea in my hands. Needless to say, I was flicking through the newspaper simultaneously.

Everyone has a talent. It could be something like dancing or singing, or perhaps even something simpler like being compassionate towards others. Mine was talking.

My speaking skills were definitely topnotch. I was mighty proud of it too. I knew what hit people's hearts, what made them cry or laugh and I said just that. Obviously, I channeled my skills for my own benefit.

It wasn't just that, but my way of speaking as well. It's all in my blood, my cabin mates used to say. I was persuasive, kind and simply charismatic. I really don't know how I did it. It all came naturally to me, and most of the times, I wasn't even aware when I was wrapping the world around my little finger with my words. I didn't know who my parents really are, though. I am an orphan, see.

I soon found what I had been looking for, a photo of myself staring back at me from the pages of the newspaper. I had given that ad to print weeks ago. I needed a job very bad. Very, very bad.

I might have been an orphan, but it wasn't like I didn't have the money to make ends meet. I was doing fine really, but I knew that the money wouldn't last forever. I had to get a secure job and quickly.

I was still looking at the photo when my phone rang. I looked at the unknown number halfheartedly. I had already received calls from many long lost friends. It had been really awkward to be bombarded with the many questions that I didn't know how to answer. I took a deep breath before taking the call and said "Hello?"

"Rachel Royce?" A lady with a firm voice asked.

"Yes, it's me."

"Hi, we have a job that we would like to offer you."

"Yes?"

"I'm sorry but we aren't allowed to disclose the job information over call. Please note this address: Room 501, Hilton Offices, Sterling Street."

I grabbed a pen and scrawled down the address.

"Come here tomorrow at 10 A.M. and we'll take it from there."

"I-" I started, but the lady had already hung up. All day that phone call remained on my mind.

This person had not even given her name. The call didn't seem official, seemingly coming from a place where fat people sit in grey suits and work seven hours a day. Hilton Offices was definitely one of those places.

By the end of the day, I was convinced that it was just a hoax, or something. Just as I was getting ready to go to bed, I noticed a message on my phone.

It was from the same unknown caller, and read:

Don't forget to bring the day's newspaper with you.

"What?" I asked aloud, looking at the message.

There wasn't anything very special in that day's newspaper, just some arguments by political leaders, a talk over a famous book and some unremarkable pieces on the rising murder rate in the city.

"How strange," I mumbled and eventually fell asleep.

There I was, standing at the reception of the office the next morning. I really needed a job and was in no mood to go home without one.

The secretary asked me, "What can I help you with?"

"Hi, I am here for the job interview and –"

"Oh, of course." Her eyes widened, as if I had just explained the Big Bang theory to her.

"I was informed to go to room 501," I explained.

"Yes, yes, that's all right, but you know, we have just heard from a very reliable source that your skills aren't quite suitable for this job. We are only accepting people who have a reputable background."

"So, you checked my background and found it unsuitable?"

She looked uncomfortable for a brief moment. "Well, you don't have a family, and-"

"What does that have to do with this job? I mentioned very specifically about my speaking skills in the ad. You should really give me a chance to at least meet someone in a position of authority before simply kicking me out of here."

"No, I am sorry, Miss Royce. It's already–"

I tuned out what she was saying and considered the situation for a moment. Whiny little secretary versus the wise me. It was a win–win situation.

I put on my best hopeless face and said, "You say that these people won't accept me because I have no one in this world, but that's exactly why I need this job so bad. No one's going to help me and this job might be the only way for me to support myself financially."

"But my boss has given orders-"

"Look, I'll tell you the truth. Right now, you're working as a secretary at the biggest office in the entire city. Someone must have chosen you for this job as well. They didn't care whether you had a family or not, did they? They considered you for your abilities and then hired you. I know that I was called here only because someone had a job that they believed I could do. Otherwise, you wouldn't have contacted me at all. Let me just speak to the people who called me here in the first place. Someone trusted you." I looked her straight in the eyes. "All I'm asking is for you to trust me as well."

The secretary pressed her lips in a thin, hard line and reluctantly revealed, "Left corridor, third room on the right." She took her seat again and resumed her work.

I stepped back, cocked my head to one side and flashed her a smile. She didn't know she'd just experienced my talent firsthand.

I followed her directions and stared at the room in front of me. 'Room 501'. I took a deep breath and walked in.

It was nothing like I had expected. The wallpaper was a bright floral one which hurt your eyes if you looked at it long enough. A faux fur sofa lay on one side, while on the other was a huge brown desk, behind which sat a lady who looked amused on seeing me. Two other people, a girl and a boy, stood on either side of her. On the desk, there was a laptop.

"Good morning, sweetheart. Have a seat." The woman smiled and motioned at a bright orange chair in front of the desk.

I sat down confused. What kind of an interview was this?

"What a performance!" She threw her head back and looked at the boy. "Didn't I tell you? She's perfect!"

"Why have you called me here?" I asked.

"Have you heard of Bluebell Publishers?" came a voice from the back of the room.

I whirled around to see a woman standing there with her arms crossed. She had a grim face and a pixie haircut to frame it.

"Well, yeah, I think so…"

She tossed something at me. It was the previous day's newspaper. The book talk was circled in red ink.

"Unknown, also known as U, is the top ranker on the New York Times bestselling list. It's written by Gwenyth Parlow, who has never yet made a public appearance. The book, Unknown, is actually a part of a trilogy, being the second book in the series. The first book, 'My Own', is tenth on the same list. We can only imagine what the last book, that is 'Torn', will do."

"What does that have to do with me?"

"Honey, this isn't a normal interview," the pixie cut woman said. "It was a test."

"Excuse me?"

"Like I said, Gwenyth Parlow has never once come out to public, has never given a single interview, or made an appearance anywhere. No one has the slightest idea of what she looks like. Until now."

The girl standing in front of me handed me a copy of the book 'Unknown'. "Last page," she whispered. I flipped the book over and saw a caricature of a woman there. I gasped.

"But, but that's my drawing! I mean, it's me!" I yelled.

Deep down, we're all someone else

2

"Calm down, honey." The woman at the back of the room walked over to my side. "We had asked Gwenyth to send us a picture of her. She sent us a drawing instead. By the time we got it, it was all smudged and crumpled. We asked our artist to do the best he could to recreate it. You know, to make it a bit pretty and presentable. That idiot copied a picture from the newspaper instead. It does not look exactly like it, but he took the main features from it and made some deliberate changes."

I looked at the cartoon closely. There was a tiny mole on the left cheek, an elaborate hairstyle and different eyebrows.

"By the time we realized this fact, they had already printed the book *with* the cartoon. All we could do then was to pay the artist to keep his mouth shut, and search for you. Obviously, we had to check your background a little. All we could find on you was that you are an orphan, but with great public speaking skills," she smirked at me. "Always first in debates, elocution, and extempore - you really are a little performer, eh? It was good news for us, anyway. *Definitely* good news."

"But that secretary-"

"I instructed her to say all that junk. I wanted to see how you would react, whether you really could convince people if you wanted. And voila! That's exactly what you did. We all were watching you through this laptop the entire time."

"Now, we would like to offer you the job!" the woman behind the desk burst out.

The pixie cut woman shot her a look. "Yes, that's what we'd like to do."

"What kind of a job?" I asked, my mind racing.

"Whoa, hey!" the boy said. "Isn't she supposed to answer some questions before-"

"Yes, yes." The pixie cut woman turned to look at me.

"You're an orphan right?"

"Yes."

"No relatives?"

"No."

"Do you trust your words to get you out of any situation?"

"Yes."

"Any?" she stressed.

I looked her in her eye and said, "I have complete trust in my skills."

Pixie cut took at long look at me.

"Are you ready to be Gwenyth Parlow?" she grinned.

I took a double-take.

"Sweetheart, you'd be puh-fect!" Sophia cooed.

"It's a chance of a life time," Pixie cut said. "You will be the public face of Gwenyth Parlow. You'll need to read all of her books cover–to-cover and we'll train you on how to answer interviews, appear in public, etc."

I was stunned, totally stunned.

"You're already such a natural at talking and stuff. So it shouldn't be too hard for you," the girl said in excitement.

"But remember," Pixie cut added, "If you accept this, you will henceforth be Gwenyth Parlow to the entire world. Only the four people in this room and you, obviously, will know the truth."

"Why exactly are you doing this?" I asked incredulously.

"The trilogy, also known as MOUT, is the next big thing after Harry Potter. It has shaken up the entire planet, the books are that mind-blowing. If people learn that Gwenyth has never even stepped out into her city, or has never had her picture taken, how will they react? BAD NEWS! From what I've heard, she is this senile old woman who spends her days washing clothes. We can't give the public that image now, can we? Instead, you will act as her."

"And how does she feel about that?" I asked, biting my lip.

The girl handed me a contract.

"It says that Gwenyth has absolutely no problem with someone else appearing as her public face. None."

I quickly skimmed my gaze over the document. "What's this other language written over here?" I questioned.

"Oh, that's just her native language. She insisted on having the contract drafted both in English and her native language," Pixie cut rolled her eyes.

"You will also be getting a salary of $5,000/month," the lady behind the desk said pointedly.

That was enough to convince me. A smile crept on my face and slowly turned into a grin. Pixie cut grinned back at me. "What about it, honey? Ready for a life of fame and fortune?"

"You bet,"I answered. And I never looked back.

~

Rachel Royce disappeared under a thick layer of makeup and a carefree attitude. I emerged a new person with a different personality.

Pixie cut, whose actual name is Zara, trained me on how to handle reporters, fans and that sort of stuff. The lady behind the desk, Sophia, had personally edited the first two books and gave me a heads-up on how to answer questions based on the story. The boy and the girl, Jake and Ashley, showed me the ropes on basic etiquettes.

"Smile shyly whenever there ask you questions related to your books. Thank the fans and give them autographs as if they are your own. I want you to practice doing that wherever you go!" Zara barked.

Even today, when I reach into my purse, at least one napkin drops out with a 'G. Parlow' scrawled over it.

"The characters of the MOUT trilogy are all different. Think about them through your daily life. What would *they* do? How would *they* react to a situation? Remember this and you will do fine," Sophia smiled.

"Smile, smile and smile! Grin, grin and grin! Just remember this simple mantra: smile till you are senile and grin till you win! You'll do amazing, Gwen!" Ashley squealed.

"Yeah, Gwen, and please don't yawn or tap your feet when in an interview. Look interested," Jake said.

Rachel was gone. Everybody now called me Gwenyth (courtesy of Zara). It was all 'Do this so you look like Gwen' and 'act like Gwen'. How did I feel about this, though? I felt awesome!

My first public appearance did go a bit rocky, though.

The interviewer had a distracting amount of gel in his hair; I personally thought that I could use some too. My own hair had been dyed, styled and was stiff with hair spray. My eyes had contact lenses on them and my eyebrows gave the impression that I was permanently raising them. When he asked, "Where have you been all this time?" I answered smoothly, "Hibernating. All that writing really got to me!"

The audience laughed and whistled at my answer. According to Zara, Gwenyth Parlow had a sarcastic and rebellious personality, quite like one of the main characters in her story.

Everything was going perfectly fine until I messed up a little bit.

"Who is your favorite character?" a fan asked.

"Well, it's Sam," I blurted out without thinking, "He's cool and calm, as well as level-headed."

"That's *not* what you were supposed to say! You had to say that you liked them all equally because they all are unique in their own special way!" Zara yelled at me afterwards.

"I know, I know!" I answered, biting my lip. I *did* like Sam the best. But 'Sam' was Rachel's answer, *not* Gwenyth's. "I am sorry, okay?"

Zara rolled her eyes at me, as if that word didn't mean anything to her.

I felt angry at myself. I hardly ever said the wrong thing, so this was a big blow for me. I decided that I would just have to work harder to suppress the Rachel in me and act more like

Gwenyth. There was no way I could afford to screw up again.

"But you were wonderful dear! Don't mind this one mistake, the rest was fantastic!" Sophia said. "Right, Zara?"

"Well, yeah, it was." Zara looked me, her expression unreadable. "Seriously, I shouldn't have pounced on you like that. Here's the contract, anyway."

The contract which Zara handed to me mentioned that I was not supposed to disclose to anyone that I wasn't the real Gwenyth Parlow. It also said that if I did, Bluebells Publishers wouldn't hold any liability for it.

I signed it (with my real signature) and handed it back to Zara.

"Great," she smiled and walked out of the room.

"OMG, you were amazing out there!" Ashley gushed.

"Thanks," I said.

Jake smiled at me for a second and then returned to being grim faced again.

By the end of the first month, I had given two interviews and had used up $5000 of my salary to buy myself some nice dresses, while saving the rest.

I was happy. Really, very happy. I lay down on my bed, smiling happily and thought, "I'm going to get used to this!!"

I felt ecstatic despite the fact that had to read the entire manuscript of Torn (700 pages) by the next day, practice with Zara, Ashley and Jake, and manage to take some time out to eat three meals between all this. But I couldn't wait!

I sighed contentedly and switched off the light, thinking that nothing could go wrong.

But that's exactly what happened, of course.

Looking in the mirror, hating the image

3

After six months of all this, I felt somewhat less enthusiastic. I came to realize that there were some serious flaws in what I had thought to be a fool-proof plan.

Firstly, I couldn't go anywhere without fans mobbing around me. I'd barely step out of my flat when some idiot would yell, "Hey! Gwenyth Parlow!"

I had changed my residence and moved to a huge penthouse, which was almost triple the size of my tiny flat. Because of that stupid contract, however, I didn't have any friends, nor could I make any new ones or invite them to the flat. I didn't have a social life. Despite having to interact with at least twenty people a day, I felt lonely as ever. I was tired of having to retire to a phony wig and sunglasses each time I needed to step out of my house. I was tired of working and chatting with strangers 24/7. My bulging pockets were full of money, but my heart was empty as ever.

For the first time ever, I missed Rachel Royce. To be honest, I didn't know who she was anymore. Being Gwenyth Parlow for the last six months, I had buried Rachel somewhere deep down, somewhere I doubted I could ever reach again. Her plain and boring life attracted me, but I was sure I would never be satisfied going to my old ways, either.

Being famous and rich had certainly grown on me. I was now being paid $10,000 per month, but I really didn't care. Even if I did, I wasn't sure about it. I yearned for someone to call me Rachael again. I wanted to call up one of my orphanage friends, see how they were getting on, but the contract had bounded me in a prison I could never escape.

This identity crisis started to really get to me. I would stare at the mirror for hours at a stretch, wondering if the girl staring back was Gwenyth or Rachel.

Then there was the issue of feeling guilty. After reading all the books of the MOUT trilogy, I felt downright ashamed of myself.

How and why did I ever, ever agree to impersonate someone just to get a taste of *their* success, fame and fortune?

None of this could rightfully be called mine. The MOUT trilogy made me laugh and cry at the same time. It made me want to scream and yell and throw things. The books were heart breaking, yet they fixed a lot of things at the same time. They explored big ideas like discrimination, sacrifice and self discovery. Selfishness, as well. The last book, Torn, had the most perfect ending to the entire trilogy. It was going to hit the stands the next month, something I was *not* looking forward to at all.

Then one day, I showed up an hour late for an interview. Things were bad enough already, but they went downhill even faster when I couldn't recall what character the lady was talking about. I could only manage to say to the retro cat-eyed woman, "I'm sorry, I'll finish this interview some other time." The interviewer was certainly surprised but let me go politely, while the crowd yelled and cameras flashed behind me. I knew that each person had paid $500 just to hear me live. Zara, of course, wasn't pleased.

"What the hell did you just do out there? You-were-supposed-to-TALK! Couldn't you do that one little thing? I can't believe that you-"

"Then don't believe it! Just freaking don't!" I yelled back, tearing at my hair.

"Don't you dare talk to me like that! You little-"

"Little? Me, Zara? Little?" I scoffed. "I'm world famous, while you are a nobody! Not me!"

"Shut up, just shut up! Don't forget that you are just pretending to be Gwenyth Parlow! You're a phony, Rachel Royce. You get that? A Fake! Without her, you are NOTHING!"

I was about to answer back when I saw Jake enter. He came up to me and gently said, "Let's go."

"No!" I yelled, even though I didn't want to stay in the room and argue with Zara anymore.

Zara pushed her hair out of her face. "Don't bother, Gwenyth. I'll go," she sneered viciously and left the room.

I collapsed into a chair. My head ached and I just wanted to leave everything. Jake handed me a glass of water. I downed it angrily and threw it at the floor, where it smashed into tiny, sharp pieces.

"Rest," Jake commanded. "That's what you need. I will come back later. Okay?"

I stared ahead, resisting the urge to hit him.

"Hello? I hope you heard me." He kneeled in front of me. "Rachel?"

I blinked, taken aback by the sound of my name. "Okay," I said and he walked out of the room with a grim face, closing the door behind him.

I tumbled onto the sofa and fell into a deep, wonderful sleep.

What if…If then…Then what?

4

I woke with a start. Maybe the interview had just been a nightmare, I thought. It was then that I noticed the shattered pieces of the glass lying on the floor.

I was in my own room at the Hilton Offices. It was exactly like Sophia's, but instead of a desk, I had my own dressing table as well as a huge wardrobe.

I changed quickly, putting on a large hat and sunglasses. I grabbed my phone and a purse. It wasn't my *own* phone – Zara had given it to me. She had confiscated my phone and smashed it with a hammer so I would never be able to get in touch with any of my old friends. Zara was the one who gave me the new flat to reside in too. My old apartment had completely been stripped of its warmth and every memory had been destroyed, including my photos, the furniture and a few belongings that I owned and loved.

I left the room and started walking, careful to hide my face. I didn't know where to go. My penthouse was one of the places I considered going to, but I had been noticing something strange for the last few days. Two men had started to follow me wherever I went. At first, I thought it was my imagination, but then I realized that they tailed after me when I wasn't at Hilton Offices or when I was out giving an interview. In fact, I think they lived just below my house. I was obviously scared and decided to talk to Jake about it, who seemed to be the only person who understood what I was going through.

I went to his room, which actually had been a storage area. Nevertheless, Jake has converted it to a space worth sitting in. "Hey, Rachel." Jake stood up on seeing me.

"We have to talk..." I started.

"Let's get outta here." Jake said, heading for the door.

~

Fifteen minutes later, we both were sitting at a nearby café. I came wearing a wig on Jake's insistence and felt very awkward. "So, Rachel," he shook his head. "Where should I start?"

"Tell me everything," I replied, looking straight at him. "Why in the world did they want me to be Gwenyth Parlow?"

"The package arrived last year. At first, it wasn't taken seriously at all, of course. When books are sent to publishing houses, they are just dumped onto a huge pile. Bluebell publishers was just starting out at that time and when people send stories like this without prior notice, letters just sit there until someone gets some time off to read them. A young editor, who was new to the house at that time, was given the task of sifting through those letters. He was very excited for the job, but after reading through around ten stories he realized how boring the task actually was. Most stories had no uniqueness, no originality. Then he picked up a dusty envelope and read the thick manuscript inside. He forwarded it to his senior editor immediately and was complimented for having spotted such brilliance. This young editor hoped that he would be given that book to edit, but it was given to another senior editor. The book was 'My Own', and the senior editor was…is…Sophia."

"And the young editor?" I asked, even though I had a hunch who it might be.

"It was me," Jake replied flatly. "I would have loved to edit it really- I mean, who wouldn't?" he looked into the distance sadly. "But Sophia was nice. She allowed me to assist her with the book, taking notes, making them. Communicating with the author, that was something else."

"What do you mean?" I asked, confused.

"Gwenyth Parlow, her handwriting is beautiful. Long and thin, neat and tidy. Her words are the real asset, though. The way she thinks; I can't believe how well she understands human nature. She's old and has lived with so many different people through her life, so I guess that does give her an advantage while writing. I wrote to her a few times, when Sophia asked me to, during the editing process. It was nice but…I just wished that-?"

"*Yours* was the name to be published as the editor, right?"

"Well, yeah. Sophia is really kind, don't get me wrong. She even told the EIC, the Editor-in-Chief, what a good job I was doing. But ever since I first read 'My Own', I've wished for that book to be mine."

"Selfishness," I sighed. "It's what tears the soul apart. You can't understand that better after reading the MOUT trilogy."

"But there is something unusual too. Gwenyth Parlow lives in an isolated little village somewhere in the hills. It isn't very far away, but she always took a long time to respond, for whatever reason. Her letters took at least a week to arrive and that slowed down the process, painfully. And she's the kind of person who talks in circles, explains everything but never really gets to the point. She sounded naïve and vulnerable, and that's where Bluebell Publishers decided to take advantage of the situation."

My eyes widened in reflex upon hearing this bit of news. I knew that whatever was coming next was going to be even more revolting.

"The President, Matthew Wells, asked Sophia to show him all the letters and every bit of communication that she had had with the author. He considered the situation and realized that he had struck a gold mine. The first thing he did was to order Sophia to send Gwenyth a letter, announcing the royalty that she would be given." He looked angry suddenly. "Try and guess the amount."

"Well, I think she should have been paid about $15,000 for that book. But I guess the publishers only paid her…" I paused to think, "$6000?"

"Wrong!" Jake snapped. "They paid Gwenyth only $4000."

I gasped. "Only $4000 for the 'My Own' book? The book that shook the planet?" Jake, however, didn't seem shocked at all. I sensed that his anger wasn't directed at me, but at Matthew Wells.

"And guess what?" Jake paused, but before I could respond, he burst out, "They told Gwenyth that the contract would quote $10,000, and $6000 from it would go to the Publishing House."

"That's barbaric!" I yelled. "How, and…" I closed my eyes, trying to process all this information. "And Gwenyth didn't say *anything*?" I asked.

"Not a word," Jake sighed deeply as I peered at him from over the rim of my glasses. It looked as if someone had let all the air and anger out of him.

He looked deflated and defeated at the same time. "Gwenyth doesn't have any idea about what's happening. She's just doing what they are asking her to."

"They?" I looked at Jake in a questioning manner.

"We. I mean all of us, really. It's not her fault either, but why can't she just come to the city and see what's happening?" Jake grabbed a napkin from the holder and began shredding it to pieces.

"I think she just wants to get her books published, so that the world can read them. I don't think it's about the money for her at all," I said carefully.

"Unlike some people here," Jake replied instantly, and I knew that this comment was directed at me.

"What I don't understand, Jake, is how you came to know of her age. I mean, just a little while ago you mentioned that she is old and has had plenty of experience with different types of people," I said, after having pondered over it for a long moment.

Jake rubbed his eyes and looked at me directly. "Gwenyth did send Sophia a picture of her. Rachel, seriously, I can't tell you how ugly it was; two front teeth missing, wild hair, and a huge mole on her left cheek. The weirdest thing is, we had asked her for a photograph and she sent us a sketch. How the heck were we supposed to publish that in the book? We did, however, ask the artist to do the best he could, but he—"

"Copied my picture instead," I finished.

"Well yeah," Jake said.

A heavy silence followed after Jake's reply and neither of us broke it.

Why? Because I said so, hon.

-Zara Wells

5

The next day when I went to work, I could tell that everyone was trying really hard to pretend that Zara and I never had the fight. They were also acting as if I had not screwed up the interview so badly. Oh, and how can I forget the fact that no one had asked after, or even mentioned, my early departure. Or Jake's, for that matter.

To cut short, some terrific acting was going on at the Hilton Offices. Someone had planned quite a show.

That 'someone' came up to me and said, "Sweetheart, let's forget about our little disagreements. We're going to have to set our differences aside and work together, right? So let's get this show on the road, honey!" Her smile seemed even sweeter than her talk.

I smiled and mimicked her tone, "Oh Zara, everything's been forgotten!"

Fat chance.

Although Zara had warned everyone in advance to not mention our fight, it didn't stop them from throwing me weird glances and breaking into whispers as soon as I left the room.

I went for the day's interviews, of course. I smiled till my cheeks hurt and answered questions on Sam and the other characters, and how Torn was going to end.

"Well, I can't reveal how it ends, obviously. That's for me to know and you to read and find out!" I winked at the crowd and flashed them a gorgeous smile.

Then I noticed Jake standing at the corner of the crowd and it wiped the smile off my face pretty fast. Luckily for me, the lady wrapped up the interview just then. The crowd hooted and yelled.

Afterwards, I realized what an image Zara had created for Gwenyth Parlow. A social butterfly, as far as writers go, she was also loud, cool and witty.

Somedays it seemed really hard to imagine that I was the pseudo-face of Gwenyth Parlow. It seemed like an enormous joke. To me, that is. The rest of the world had accepted this fact and was happily watching our show. Or was it my show?

The thing is, it's really easy to fool the world. Put on a mask, talk smoothly and everyone will eat out of your hand. But the question is, how long can you keep fooling yourself?

I had got my answer the previous day from Jake. The answer was, and still is, simple: you can't.

~

Torn's release date was drawing closer. Sophia and Ashley were buzzing with excitement, while Zara looked a bit grim. Jake had his own anger slowly building up.

A few days before Torn hit the stands was going to be the day of my last interview. Zara thought it was best to do this to prevent the heat and the hype from dying down.

Ha, ha.

The interviewer was a nice and friendly person whom I had seen on TV quite a few times before. He cracked me up with his remarks and asked me questions related to my social background, my daily routine, and of course MOUT.

Questions related to my so-called life weren't difficult at all, since I had rehearsed them with Zara a million times. Then he asked an extremely queer question.

"So do you ever feel like Jane while writing these books? Or do you feel like Gwenyth Parlow?" He winked at the enormous crowd.

At first, my heart started beating fast. I thought that my truth had been revealed, as if someone had seen through my masquerade and announced that I wasn't actually Gwenyth, but Rachel Royce.

The crowd broke into laughter and whistles and I blinked, realizing that the man had only been joking. Jane was one of the characters of MOUT who lives in a remote village and is an aspiring but failed writer. At the end of 'Unknown', she bumps into Sam and realizes that he looks familiar. That is where the book abruptly ends. The MOUT is narrated from the viewpoints of its different characters, and when Jane narrates, she can make even a sunny day seem gloomy. She's a pessimist, but one can't help but love her for some reason.

"Jane is my loveliest creation. She's selfish, moody and evil, but there is another side to her. I don't feel like Jane while writing, but sometimes even Gwenyth gets lost trying to guess how Jane would feel. Aah! Even the greatest souls don't have a map to guide them around, what can one expect from a mere mortal?" I finished, smiling mysteriously and bowed slightly at the people.

The audience went wild. They loved my answer so much they started cheering, "Gwenyth! Gwenyth!" and I could still hear those chants reverberating in my head as I walked back into my room at the Hilton Offices. I was grinning to myself, happy with my performance, when Jake entered.

His face looked awful. His eyes bore into mine and he seemed to have steam coming out of his ears. He looked furious.

"Hi, Jake!" I chirped brightly. "I killed it today, like totally, right?"

"Of course, you *did,*" he replied, making it sound like a threat.

"I know. I mean, everyone was clapping for me, hooting and whistling…it felt so good," I replied dreamily. "You saw it, Jake. Tell me how awesome it was!"

"Awesome?!" Jake spat.

"Yeah, Jake!" I grinned. "I was a-ma-zing!" Jake kicked the chair in front of him. "You were amazing. Okay? Is that enough? Or do you want that to be in tomorrow's newspaper?"

I was confused. "Jake, chill. People loved me. They clapped and cheered-"

"And you don't deserve any of it! You know that? It's Gwenyth who deserves all of it!"

"Jake, you don't understand," I shook my head because he really didn't. "They were chanting my name too and-"

"They were not chanting YOUR name! Or have you changed it? Have you forgotten so soon?"

I felt absolutely flabbergasted while Jake yelled.

"You are Rachel, not Gwenyth! Remember, *Rachel Royce*?" he sneered.

Rachel…Rachel. That little word burst my bubble.

Of course, how could I've forgotten? I wasn't Gwenyth. I was never Gwenyth, I was Rachel. Jake was right, I didn't deserve even a bit of that applause or cheering. I suddenly lost my balance and crashed down, hard. My high heels felt broken and my head reeled. A sob escaped my throat.

I realized that I was indeed just Rachel Royce, a little wannabe who got famous by fluke. I wasn't Gwenyth and I could never be her, no matter how hard I tried to fool myself. I pressed my face against the floor and cried.

Impulsiveness is what we most regret

6

After some time, I regained my composure and sat up, shaking slightly. I kicked off those heels and stood up, swaying. Jake was still there, sitting with his face in his hands. I went over to the dressing table and started pulling clips out of my hair, one by one.

"Jealous, aren't you, Jake?" I asked him, staring at his reflection in the mirror. "That I'm the one who's getting all the claps and cheers without having done anything?"

Jake looked up and replied in a defeated voice.

"Yes."

I blinked. I hadn't expected him to admit it so easily. I continued tugging at my hair.

"I want to meet Gwenyth Parlow," I said, loud and clear.

"Of course, you do," came Jake's cryptic reply.

"Zara told me that I would be free to do anything after I give the last interview perfectly and that's exactly what I did. And now, both of us are going to go meet Gwenyth, and-"

"What then?" Jake questioned.

"Well, we'll tell her what's been going on and hear her side of the story. We'll have to explain it nicely to her because she's old. Who knows what she'll do," I finished confidently.

"Hmm. You're on your own though," Jake said in a conclusive tone.

"What? Why? Don't you-? I mean, aren't you coming with me?" I asked.

"I don't want to, and even if I did, I wouldn't be able to. Zara's given leave to you, not me. But I support you wholeheartedly. I'll give you Gwenyth's address and stuff, and make all the necessary arrangements, okay?" Jake looked at me.

"Fine, I guess. It would be nice if you come along too," I added hastily.

"I'll see, okay?" Jake sounded exasperated. "You don't want to face Gwenyth alone, right?"

I pulled a face and then sighed, "You're right. I don't know *what* I'll say to her, *how* I'll face her...gosh!"

"Chill out. I'll see if I can convince Zara, but you know how she is."

"What does Zara exactly do, anyway? Who appointed her as my...um...mentor, or whatever?"

The reply Jake gave me answered much more than what I had asked for.

"She's Matthew Wells' daughter, Zara Wells."

~

The day after my last interview, I found myself sitting in complete silence at my penthouse. The furniture, the floor, everything that had seemed alien before, was now a familiar sight. "Don't get too used to it," I said aloud, warning myself. I poured myself a cup of coffee and switched on my laptop. I typed in 'Gwenyth Parlow' and my own photos flooded the screen instantly, along with a list of awards that I had got—I mean that *Gwenyth* had got.

I tried to find Gwenyth's address, but no website had the slightest clue regarding where she lived. The internet contained every other information, except for what I was looking for.

I shut the laptop down. I then went to the bathroom and stood in front of the mirror. There stood a girl, confident and strong, with a slightly shy look on her face. Brown hair, curved eyebrows and a small smile. Then the image changed. The girl in front of me looked tired, with dark bags hanging under her eyes. Her hair was perfectly straight and of a blondish color, her eyebrows had a mysterious arch. She looked absolutely defeated. I touched the mirror with a trembling hand and she did the same. *This* was who I had become. Lost on the inside, Gwenyth on the outside. The other girl was just a mirage. Bur she was also Rachel Royce.

I knew that there was only one way to bring her back to life and it was by meeting the real Gwenyth Parlow; by bringing her justice and all that she truly deserved, by *punishing* those who had robbed her of her fame and fortune.

'Those' meaning Matthew Wells, Bluebell Publishers, Zara, etc.

And myself.

~

"Here's Gwenyth's address," Jake said, handing me a piece of paper. "Don't ask me how I got it."

"Okay," I said, taking the paper on which Jake had scrawled the address. "501, Greenwood Avenue. Shalom Hills," I read the address. "Shalom Hills? Isn't that, like, a village somewhere in those mountainous regions?"

"Yep, that's right," Jake said. "It'll take us-"

"Us?" I questioned.

"I somehow persuaded Zara to give me a day off," Jake answered.

"Wow, I mean—how did you do it?"

"Zara's already pretty excited about Torn hitting the stands. I convinced her that there is nothing we can do now but to just wait and watch. I'm leaving with you tomorrow."

"OMG, thank you so much, Jake." I heaved a sigh of relief.

"I've asked Ashley to cover for me and Sophia to not mention my absence, so it's all cool. I've also told Ash what we're doing," Jake added.

"What?!"

"Ash is fine, she won't tell anyone. I figured we could do with someone on the inside, who's close to both Zara and Sophia," Jake explained.

"Are you sure that we can trust Ashley?" I asked.

"Positive. So tomorrow, you and I will leave for the town by bus and find Gwenyth. It'll take us about two hours to reach there, but we'll have to walk a lot. What will we do once we find Gwen though?"

"We'll tell her how Bluebells has been taking advantage of her. We'll explain how I've been her public image all this while, and-" I stopped short.

"And?" Jake pressed.

"After the release of Torn, there'll be this huge event which will cover the entire trilogy. Maybe we can invite Gwen to it and reveal the truth to the world. I don't care if she's old and has two missing teeth. She deserves all this money and fame," I explained.

Jake looked at me keenly for a long time.

"You know, I think you're onto something, Rachel. It's a great idea and it's worth a shot." He smiled at me.

"So it's settled then," I concluded.

"I used to think before that you are an incredibly selfish person to be taking someone else's fame and credit for things that you had not done. But I think very differently now," Jake added.

"It has always been different, Jake. Before this Gwenyth Parlow thing, I was just an ordinary orphan who wanted a job. I was never very social and living in an orphanage cut me off in a way from the real world. So when I got this offer to be rich and famous with hardly any effort at all, I jumped at the chance, not that I had much choice at that time anyway," I explained.

"It's nice to know you, Rachel," Jake smiled and walked away.

I took the elevator to success!

-Matthew Wells

7

The next morning, I was up and ready within fifteen minutes. Jake had messaged me the name of the bus station where we were going to meet and I stood there, patiently waiting for him to arrive. Just then, my phone rang and I picked it up. "Hello?"

"Rachel? It's me, Jake."

"Jake, I'm here waiting for-"

"Sorry, Rachel. I can't come with you to meet Gwenyth. I'll explain later. Ashley will be going with you."

"Jake, but why? I mean-"

"I'm sorry, Rachel. I can't face Gwenyth, sorry."

Jake hung up.

I was confused and angry at Jake. *He couldn't meet Gwenyth? Why? Why not? And how—*

My thoughts were interrupted by the sound of Ashley's voice. "Hey Rachel, let's get going," she smiled at me.

We boarded the bus that would take us to Shalom Hills. Ashley stared at me with a strange look on her face. I decided to ignore her and look out the window, but it was starting to creep me out.

I got really self-conscious and I asked,"What?" Ashley smiled and dismissively waved her hand.

"Nothing, I was just surprised when Jake said that meeting Gwenyth was your idea. Especially after the contract you had signed."

I gave her a strange look. "The contract said I couldn't reveal my true identity to anyone, and if I did, Bluebells wouldn't have anything to do with it."

Ashley shook her head slightly as if to say 'Duh!' and confessed, "That's the whole point, isn't it? You will be alone in this if the whole world learns the truth. Bluebells will simply back out of it."

"Well..." I had thought this out already. If Bluebells were to back out, then so be it. I had decided that after I convinced Gwenyth to come, she would tell everyone that she had been receiving a mere amount of $4000 per month for her books. The news channels were always going on how MOUT was selling like hot cakes and Gwenyth was going to be a millionaire...no, billionaire. Gwenyth would believe me (I hoped) and she'd be *so* grateful to me that she'd forgive me (I *really* hoped) and save me from all the lawsuits and other such consequences.

I realized I hadn't given Ashley an answer still but she continued talking. "Jake will help you expose Bluebells Publishers, won't he?"

"What?" I asked right back.

"He didn't tell you, did he?" Ashley questioned.

"Tell me *what*?" It seemed that Ashley and I were answering each other's questions with questions, which was getting on my nerves.

"Bluebells Publishers was actually started by Jake's father," Ashley finally explained. "It was a decently good company with some hit books. Everything was fine, really, until Matthew Wells joined. Matthew Wells is-"

"Zara's father, I know," I interrupted.

"Right. So, I'm not sure *exactly* what happened but Matthew backstabbed Jake's father and kicked him out of his own company. Jake's father, well, went into depression, and-" Ashley tilted her head in a non-committal way. I nodded at her indication, utterly shocked.

"Jake became thirsty for revenge. He joined Bluebells, but soon after, Matthew became the president and made Zara his assistant or something. Now they're just looking for a reason to throw Jake out of the company too," she finished, biting her lip.

I stared out of the window, letting everything sink in. *Jake's father started Bluebells? No wonder Jake was so eager to participate in this plan.*

"What does Zara do, exactly?" I asked.

"Well, I think she just hangs around to keep an eye on Jake. All the others really like him, but

Zara's just waiting for Jake to make a mistake. She's got better chances now too, since she was made the agent."

"Excuse me? Who's agent?"

"Oh, you don't know?" Ashley asked right back.

Enough was enough. I decided to not repeat our question-to-question session all over again.

"No, I don't know and would be incredibly pleased if you told me," I gritted my teeth.

Ashley sensed my annoyance. "Sorry. After the first book of MOUT, Matthew Wells told Sophia to send Gwenyth a letter proclaiming that Zara was her agent."

"What?! If she had already published her first book, why did she require an agent?" I half-shouted. "Isn't the job of the agent to get the book published?"

"Yes and no. Sometimes writers hire literary agents after their books get published to manage their career and help them make better decisions. For example, if an author isn't happy with how his first book performed, he can hire an agent. The agent will then find a better publishing company with better editors, so the book can fetch better results," Ashley explained.

"Care to tell me *why* anyone would hire an agent who is connected with the same darn company to find better publishing houses?" I snapped.

Ashley looked very calm. "I know that, you know that, but Gwenyth didn't, and Wells-"

"Took advantage of the situation!" I yelled.

"Yes," Ashley confirmed placidly.

I balled up my fists and thought, "Matthew and Zara Wells are going down, down, DOWN!"

~

The bus dropped us at Shalom Hills. It had been a rough ride and Ashley was relived to pursue the rest of the journey on foot.

"So..." Ashley said, "What's next? How are we going to find Gwenyth?"

"We'll have to find Greenwood Avenue first. Let's just ask the locals where it is," I replied, mentally rolling my eyes at her question. Before I had finished talking, Ashley had already bounded off. I could hear her asking a local cheerfully, "Hi! Do you know where Greenwood Avenue is?"

I didn't hear the reply though, because the man had been standing with his back to me. "Come along, I know where it is," Ashley gesticulated at me to follow her.

Shalom Hills was a tiny and simple looking town. I was surprised that a bus even went there in that season because there were hardly any tourists around.

Ashley led the way. We turned right from the bus station and went straight past the main market, turning into narrow alley on the left.

"Are you sure we're going the right way?" I asked, convincing yet another shawl seller that I didn't want to purchase anything.

"Yep," Ashley was firm in her reply but a needle of doubt still persisted.

We walked some more and suddenly, Ashley stopped and announced, "This is it."

I stared at where she had bought us.

"But, but…this is a ropeway!" I spluttered.

Ashley grinned at me. "Guess we'll find Gwen in the clouds then."

We hustled into the trolley and watched the town below us grow tinier and tinier.

"Turns out that the habitation at the top of the hill also comes within Shalom Hills," she said.

We climbed out and I gave Ashley a questioning look.

"Come on," she beckoned and I quickly followed behind. She turned left, went straight and turned left again. I give her credit for remembering the directions perfectly.

"Look!" Ashley pointed as we came to a stop in front of a row of small colorful houses. An old lady was just stepping out of the first one.

Her wild hair and the huge mole were achingly familiar.

"Oh my God, it's her! Gwenyth Parlow!" Ashley screamed.

Both of us ran up to the woman. She looked at us with a confused look on her face.

"Are you Gwenyth Parlow? Gwenyth Parlow?" Ashley asked.

I couldn't open my mouth, let alone speak. My entire body felt like a giant rock, stiff and impossible to move.

"Who iz zat?" The woman asked sharply. I couldn't place her accent. "Why zo you want to know?"

"We're from the Publishing Company. *You* are Gwenyth Parlow, right?"

The woman (Gwenyth?) opened her mouth immediately, but suddenly stopped, hesitating.

"Go on," Ashley said, egging her on.

The woman replied "I haven'tz heard of any Gwenyth Parlow."

~

The woman was lying. She had to be.

The picture description Jake had given me matched her perfectly. Here was the woman, standing right in front of us, who was supposed to be Gwenyth Parlow, but wasn't actually her? It was insane.

Suddenly, a thought struck me. *What if the woman knew Gwenyth Parlow, but was lying through her teeth for some reason?*

I also didn't like the way she was nervously scratching her neck, looking away. I had a sudden burst of inspiration.

"Well, that's too bad. Isn't it, Ashley?" I asked facing her, while the woman looked up with interest. "We had come all this way to give money to Gwenyth Parlow, and now we can't find her." I sighed deeply. "Thanks anyway," I said to the woman who had been staring at me with her eyes wide open, and turned to leave. Ashley followed suit.

"Wait, wait!" the woman yelled. Ashley and I exchanged glances and turned around to face the woman again.

"I…I am Gwenyth Parlow," she said. "I did not say it before as I thought zat maybe you all have found out zat-" she rambled, suddenly stopping short. Her face grew pale.

"Oh, so *now* you remember," Ashley rolled her eyes.

"What did you think we found out? Huh?" I snapped. "Tell us!"

"Iz was by accident! I said, by accident!" She waved her hands, as if trying to defend herself.

I pulled out my driver's license from my pocket and flashed it close to her face. "We're police!" I yelled. "Now tell us what you know or-"

"You-know-what!" Ashley joined in.

We had scared the marbles out of the old woman. She started, going on muttering in another language.

"ENGLISH!" I screamed.

"I not know—I didn't zo anything—it waz her-ze girl…"

"What girl!?" Ashley asked.

"Who leeves in zat house!" she screamed, pointing down the road. "She wrote ze story, zat's all…I just handzeled everything…iz not my fault!" she heaved, but Ashley and I had already started running towards the house which she had pointed to. As I came closer to it, I realized it said '501'.

"This is Greenwood Avenue!" Ashley yelled.

"I know!" I replied.

We pounded on the door. My heart raced and my insides tingled at the thought of finally coming face-to-face with the real Gwenyth. A sudden heaviness came upon me, making it hard to breathe, as the door slowly opened.

There stood a girl, extremely thin with thick long hair, a shade of blonde so light that they almost looked white. Her dress floated around her, evidently larger than her size. Her face reflected innocence, with big round eyes and a timid expression.

"Are you—I mean, did you write MOUT?"

The girl looked confused. "My name is Shaila Faye," she said.

"No, did you write My Own, Unknown and Torn?" Ashley asked.

The girl looked at us for a long painful moment. Her answer sounded like shattering glass, painful, but it was music to my ears at the same time.

"Yes, I did."

Some thoughts ought to remain just thoughts

8

Time stopped for me at that moment. Not like they show in the movies, when everything moves in slow-motion, or when every sound goes mute; time just decided to break the rules for *me* as I stood there, hearing every little sound, my breath, my heartbeat, and taking in every little detail, like how rough Gwenyth's hands were and how her eyes were liquid-brown with two small suns in them, and how she wore a peach-colored hearing aid. Just as suddenly as it had stopped, time resumed again. Ashley said, "We really need to talk to you." Gwenyth's face portrayed confusion, but she welcomed us inside. Ashley made me go first, as if she suspected me to make a break for it as soon as she turned her back on me.

I would never have done that. Well, maybe.

The house was tiny, but cozy. Everything had a vintage feel to it. There was a huge gramophone in one corner, along with one of those bulky red dial phones. A rocking chair rested in another corner of the room and a small light brown sofa occupied the centre.

Gwenyth led us into another room. Sunlight streamed in from one tiny window, casting a dull-lit effect in the room. The rest of the room was dark and cool.

Gwenyth pointed towards two chairs in there, and Ashley and I took a seat. Gwenyth settled herself in a wooden chair behind a wooden desk.

"Gwenyth..." Ashley started then sighed.

Usually, I would've done the talking in any situation, but I sat silently at that moment.

"Yes?" Gwenyth asked, her fingers busily toying with her dress.

Ashley seemed to be at a loss of words. She looked at me helplessly, and I knew this was the one thing that I had to do. Ashley's look clearly said, 'I memorized all those directions, but that's it. I can't do anything more.'

"My name is Rachel Royce and this is Ashley Moore. Ashley works at Bluebells and I...well, I work there too, sort of." I took a deep breath. "It all started when I got a phone call..."

The rest of the story unfolded quite quickly. It came out so fast, I wondered if I had been working on it subconsciously all this time. I watched Gwenyth as I explained. Her face displayed many emotions at the same time, so it became a mixture of all of them. Her eyes expressed surprise, her eyebrows were raised in a confused arch, her cheeks grew red and her jaw dropped open slightly. She twiddled with the hem of her dress and fidgeted with one of the black buttons on her dress a few times. She adjusted the hearing aid too, as if she couldn't believe what she was hearing.

When I finally finished, she stared at me and then looked out the window, straining her neck as if waiting for someone to come. She looked at Ashley, and then turned her gaze to me. "Weird, isn't it, how things have turned out?" she asked me.

"Um..." I was still looking for the right words to answer, when she spoke again, "Like vanilla ice-cream. Everything looks normal, but something's hidden there." She scrunched her eyebrows and tilted her head dreamily.

"Yes, so, what shall we do now?" I asked, and she immediately looked startled as if I'd thrown cold water on her.

"Now? I think it's funny you pretended to be me, Rachel!" She stood up, swishing her dress dramatically. "A real-life masquerade! A show put up right under the world's nose! I can't believe you were-are-me!" she giggled. "We don't even look alike, do we?" she asked, studying my face carefully.

"That isn't the point," I said as gently as I could manage. "I'm already pretending to be you, but what's important is what we should do next. Okay?"

"Okay." She sat down again, grinning and swinging her legs. "I have my very own-" she stopped short. "What should I call you, Rachel? You're pretending to be me, but I don't think there's a word for that. You're like my human equivalent of a pseudonym; no, no, I already have one!" she argued with herself. Her face suddenly lit up. "Got it! You're my pseudo-face. A fake face for the world...ha! Wow." She looked quite pleased with herself.

"Gwenyth-"Ashley started.

"That's not my name. It's Shaila Faye."

"Then who's Gwenyth?" I asked. She sighed and twirled around. She looked exasperated and said huffily, "I just told you, that's my pseudonym. Aunt Gwen told me to use her name, so I did." She smiled. "Aunt Gwen is really old and can't even chew her food properly because she has two of her front teeth missing. I feel really bad for her," Shaila explained.

Ashley and I looked at each other. The identity of Gwenyth Parlow - both fake and real - had finally been revealed to us.

"Shaila, will you come with us to the city?" I asked her, getting straight to the point.

Her eyes twinkled as she said, "I'd love to!"

"Great. So-"

"I've never been to the city before, not even to Shalom Hills!" She sounded upset. "I'd love to go," she repeated.

"So how did you manage to send us the story?" Ashley asked.

Shaila paused for a long moment. "Well, I wrote my stories and then my…well um…Uncle posted them to the city from the Shalom Hills' Post Office."

"Wow, I mean, that's…" Ashley started, but found herself at a loss of words to complete the sentence.

"Magical, completely!" Shaila grinned.

I smiled at Shaila. She was so childish, it seemed as if we were talking to a five year old. But she wasn't a five year old. We were talking to the person who had written the best series of books to have ever been published on the entire planet.

"Shaila, how did you write the books? Imagined the characters and everything?" Ashley asked brightly.

At that moment, I analyzed Ashley Moore in an instant. She was so naïve, not really living in the real world. Here she was, living her fan-girl moment with the best author, who was supposed to be an old lady, but turned out to be a young eccentric girl instead.

Ashley really had no idea of what to say or do at the right time. I'll admit, even I was practically biting my lip to stop myself from asking those questions which had been flooding my mind since

I heard Gwen-sorry, Shaila's 'magical, completely' remark.

As it goes, I was right.

Shaila's mouth curved into a smile. She adjusted her hearing aid and said, "Wait a minute. Let me think about that." She tapped her chin, while staring out the window for at least an entire minute. Ashley glanced at me incredulously in a 'what-did-I-do' manner. I puckered my mouth and shook my head slightly, as if saying, 'There's-nothing-to-be-done-now'.

Shaila returned her gaze to look at us. "Okay, so it all started when I got this amazing idea, and then I saw a butterfly..." she said in her quiet and dreamy voice, trailing off. "And then I started to write the story. I thought of Sam, Jane, Zack, everyone and penned them down on paper. They talked to me sometimes, Rachel. They talked to me!" she explained in a little girl's voice. Her words was full of feeling and I looked into her eyes, expecting them to twinkle or shine the way they do when one talks about something one enjoys or loves a lot.

But no. Her eyes were plain and opaque. They seemed to be trying to give off a dreamy effect, but it looked forced, almost unreal. I was beginning to feel uncomfortable listening to her ramble, so I just had to cut in.

"I feel certain that you wrote it just wonderfully," I said, not being able to figure out how to deal with Shaila. "The media will love all this…stuff (although 'junk' would have been a more appropriate description). We'll hear it all then."

"Oh…okay!" Gwen-Shaila squealed.

"Shaila, can you give me your phone number, so we can be in touch?" I asked carefully.

"Of course. It's 9838****70," she replied.

"Great. Thanks!" I said, happy at finding a way to communicate with her.

"Shaila, why did you let Gwenyth—I mean, why did you use her name as a pseudonym?" Ashley asked. I did my best to *not* roll my eyes. *Ashley strikes again! Did she really want to listen to Shaila's childish explanations?* I thought to myself.

Gwen waited, fiddling with the button on her dress.

"I told you, I felt sorry for her. She's old and she's my aunt, so…I thought this was the least I could do. Anyway, I became Gwenyth Parlow and let her sign all my contracts too!" she giggled. "I didn't read or sign a single one. My aunt did! She took all the money as well!"

"Of course," I breathed, connecting the dots slowly in my head.

"I really didn't care what happened as long as I got my story published," Shaila ended, and my heart burst with emotion for her.

"I hate to say this, but we really have got to go now," Ashley proclaimed, looking first at Shaila and then at me. "If Zara finds out about any of this, we-"

"Okay, fine," I cut in, standing up. "We'll go now. Okay, Shaila?"

"Oh…well, goodbye!" she said, delightfully waving her hand.

Ashley exited the room and I was about to follow, when I suddenly stopped in the doorway. Thinking something, I turned around and looked at Shaila, who was now peeping out of the window, as if waiting to check whether Ashley and I had left.

"Shaila," I said. She jumped on hearing her name and twirled around.

"I…" I hesitated, wanting to know and not know at the same time. I took a deep breath and finally asked, "Aren't you angry with me?"

"Why would I be-ouch!" She swatted at her ear slightly. Her peach-colored hearing aid nearly fell to the ground.

I raised my eyebrows, confused. Shaila had responded in a really rude manner. She went from being cute and kind to snappy in just a moment. She seemed to realize it too, but didn't skip a beat.

"Yes, what were you saying?" she asked in her dreamy voice.

I opened my mouth to answer, but then decided against it, realizing that if I asked my question again, I would be no different from Ashley.

"Never mind, Gwenyth," was all I could say before walking away, and this time, Shaila didn't bother to correct me.

Success is truly the best revenge.

-Jake Parker

9

Ashley and I didn't speak at all. We quietly went back to Shalom Hills and boarded a bus back home. I wanted to talk to Ashley, but as soon as we took our seats, she dozed off, evidently tired.

I was by myself yet again, but in a different kind of way this time. I wasn't feeling 'alone', but rather blissful in my solitude. I thought hard and long, carefully considering every single aspect of my situation.

Bluebells Publishers had trapped me, no doubt. But I was determined to find an escape. *My* escape.

Just like that, I formulated a foolproof plan, sitting right there in the bus, with Ashley gently snoring beside me. Only time could tell if it would work. I wondered if my strategy was good enough, but I had no doubt about my abilities as a schemer.

"Let's do it!" I thought, although slightly unsure.

Jake and I met at the same café where we had met before. It was a Sunday, so Jake had a day off. Ashley *still* had to do some last minute work for Zara, so she couldn't join us.

"So, what was it like, meeting Gwenyth Parlow?" Jake asked.

"Her real name is Shaila Faye. She's probably in her early twenties, not the old woman that you described from the picture. I know, I know," I replied, seeing Jake's astonished face and told him all about our meeting with Shaila.

"Oh My God," was all that Jake could muster to say.

"I don't understand why you couldn't come, Jake. I got pretty surprised when Ashley came instead of you," I said, careful of not overdoing it, so that it didn't sound like I was accusing him.

"I'm sorry, Gwen, I mean Rachel." Jake reddened slightly on calling me Gwen. He cleared his throat nervously. "I-I couldn't-*can't* face Gwenyth."

I sensed he had something more to say, so I waited for him to explain.

"You know all the money that Bluebells' taking? From Shaila? Most of it goes into Matthew Well's pocket, but guess where the rest of it goes? To pay *our* salaries. I can't stand it really, that I should reap the benefits of the hard work that Shaila did, but the reality is that I'm indeed getting her money. Some days, I feel like I deserve it. I've worked endless hours for Bluebells, but never felt that I got a fair wage for it. I just can't face Gwenyth. I can't face her," Jake ended with a sigh.

"I feel just like that, Jake, every single second of the day. It's like there's a time bomb that just keeps ticking…tick, tick...” I tapped a pen on the table, making an extremely annoying sound. “I've lived with this sound for the last five months or so. It'll never stop – that's what it feels like, right?” Jake's face got scrunched up, irritated with the sound. “But yesterday, when I came back from Shaila's, the sound just vanished. It vanished completely, Jake, and I can't tell you what a beautiful sleep I had last night.” I stopped the ticking. “It helps, Jake, to do the right thing. When I faced Shaila, I felt as if I would just collapse right there, or that the bomb would burst. But it didn't.”

“And that makes all the difference,” Jake concluded, looking at me. “It's all worth it.”

“Of course it is, Jake,” I replied.

We sat in silence for a while. Jake drummed his fingers listlessly.

“Ashley told me about your father,” I started. “Bluebells, Matthew, everything.”

“Oh,” Jake traced the tip of his finger over the tabletop randomly. “I was just a kid when Dad got the idea of starting a company. A few years later, he *did* and he called it Bluebells.”

“Go on,” I egged him on.

Jake opened his mouth, but soon closed it again, having second thoughts perhaps.

“I don't want to talk about it, Rachel.” He spread his fingers wide on the table. “I'm sorry.”

I nodded my head. We just waited in silence, both equally unsure of what to say next.

"So, Shaila'll be coming here?" Jake asked.

"Well, yes. After Torn releases, we will have this party, or function, whatever. I was thinking we could perhaps tell the world about Shaila then," I offered.

"Nice plan. I got the confirmation from Zara that Torn will be out on the stands next week."

"That's sooner than I had expected," I said, a swarm of butterflies beating rapidly against my chest.

"Zara really rushed the process." Jake banged his hand on the table. "She can't wait to be a millionaire!" He snapped in an angry outburst.

"Look, Jake, I-"

"I'll see you tomorrow, maybe?" Jake said, as he stood up and walked away, disappearing into the crowd.

"Fine," I whispered to myself, a plan stirring inside my head.

~

I was waiting at a mall, all dressed up with a wig, hat and sunglasses, which had become my daily essentials now.

I had messaged Jake to arrive at 6 P.M., to come meet me after leaving work. Jake arrived at 6:15, slightly puzzled.

"Yeah?" he asked, when he approached me.

"Hello to you too," I replied, tilting my head.

"Hi. Why have-"

"So, I was just thinking how we've worked our pants off for Bluebells. We truly deserve some luxuries. And I thought that we could maybe get them today," I explained with a smile.

"At a mall?" Jake questioned, his voice laced with sarcasm.

"Yes, a mall can be a very rewarding place. It has a game-zone, a theatre, a haunted house-"

"How old are we? Ten?" Jake snorted.

"We'll have fun. Ever heard of that?"

"Of course-"

"Great. Bet I can beat you at air hockey!" I challenged, which convinced Jake and we were off.

That day was the most fun-filled day I had had in a long time. We played at the Game-zone, ate at a fast-food joint, raced around in bumper cars. We laughed and screamed at the cheesy haunted house, and finally settled down with scoops of ice-cream.

"Liked it?" I asked, grinning.

Jake just smiled, licking his ice-cream. Last but not the least, I dragged Jake for a movie, which was all about the end of the world and apocalypse, but hey, we were facing something just as difficult to survive in our real lives.

We exited the mall, laughing at my weird impersonation of one of the zombies in the film.

Jake seemed elated, while I was just glad that no one else saw through my masquerade.

"Thanks for everything, Rachel. I had an awesome time."

This time, I smiled mysteriously and we parted ways, both thinking about the way things had gone that day.

Why can't things stay the same?

-Rachel Royce

10

The next day, I called Zara to ask when *exactly* was Torn hitting the stands, and when my break would get over.

"Hon, Torn's releasing in five days, right? I think you should start coming to office from the first day after Torn's release. The major interviews will start only a week after the book's out. Got it?"

"So I won't have to come before that, right?"

"Yep. Right now we are showing to the public that you've disappeared; not literally, so that the hype doesn't cool down. And then, BAM! (Zara screamed so loudly, my phone almost slipped out of my hands.) There you will be, talking about your wonderful story and thanking the crowd."

"Thank you-"

"Sweetheart, there is no need for that. Oh, Jake and Sophia made some last minute changes to the manuscript, make sure you read 'em. Ciao!" She hung up.

"Thank you for nothing, Zara!" I finally finished my sentence viciously.

For the next few days, I just relaxed at my house. Thankfully, Zara has decided not to disclose my residence to the world, so I was safe in my flat.

I carefully went through my plan over and over again. I thought about the Gwenyth who was Shaila's aunt, and about the Gwenyth who I had been portraying. I thought how ironic it all was, how one person, one name had been given such diverse personalities.

I thought of Jake, of Bluebells, Shaila and the Wells. I thought about my parents, and most importantly, about myself. How alone I was in the cruel world, which witnessed one race after the other for wealth and power, instilling envy and revenge in humans at the same time.

I analyzed Jake as best as I could and whenever we talked, it was always, 'Gwen-this, Gwen-that'. Perhaps he had something up his sleeve too.

Perhaps not.

But right at that moment, all I could do was to just wait and watch.

~

Soon came my last day of freedom. Torn was scheduled to release the next day, and I found myself sitting quietly in front of my T.V., utterly anxious. The news reporter was a young girl with straight black hair.

"In latest news, 'Torn' will be releasing today. News is buzzing that Torn will probably break all previous publishing records and become an instant hit. Let's hear it from Richard at a well-known bookstore."

The scene of a bookstore filled the screen. I gasped at what I saw.

"And as you can see right now, anticipating fans have been counting down the time left for Torn to get released. Some of the folks here have stayed overnight, camping out in the cold, just to have a copy of Torn in their hands." The crowd was unbelievable. The lines stretched all the way to the end of the block and wrapped around the bend. Some people looked absolutely frazzled.

Turning off the T.V., I grabbed my phone and quickly tapped a message. The reply came back instantly. I quickly washed, changed (putting on my daily essentials), and was out of the house in no time.

I went to Blossom's Park straight away. It had been one of my absolute favorite parks since I was very young. I stopped at the gate labeled '3' and waited patiently.

Jake walked tentatively towards me, smiling slightly. He came up to me and both of us went in for a stroll.

"So…" Jake began.

"Torn is releasing today," I said biting my lip.

"I know, You're feeling nervous, right?"

"Yes, I mean, guilty too. It's not my book, I don't deserve any of this…I feel awful," I declared.

Jake nodded, understanding. "So what's the plan with Gwenyth-Shaila?"

"Well, it's the same for now. But the thing is, I won't be able to go anywhere after tomorrow, Jake. I was thinking if you could bring Shaila here on the day of the party. We can't bring her before that."

"Why not?!" Jake asked. "It'd actually be a lot easier."

"Jake, where would Shaila stay? We can't keep her at a hotel, she's a total goofball. I could let her stay with me, but I'm pretty sure I'm being followed."

"What?" Jake questioned, and I told him about the two men.

Jake looked angry. He shook his head and said, "I can't believe Zara got two of her cronies to tail you!"

We walked in silence for a while. Two kids on their bicycles ran past us, laughing. "Jake, what exactly did happen with you and the Wells?" I asked, finally having mustered up the courage.

Jake sighed and raked his hand through his hair.

"After Dad started the company, he was joined by Matthew Wells, who eventually became Dad's partner and co-founder. That's the way it went on for some years. Then Matthew Wells got greedy. Dad was the President and he was the Vice-President, as they had mutually agreed to be, years ago. Something went really wrong and the Wells very cleverly put the entire blame on Dad, because of which everyone started suspecting him. My father couldn't really do anything, he didn't want to work in a company where no one trusted him and talked behind his back. He resigned." Jake's face had gone pale and his hands balled up in fists.

"Dad was too good a person to fight or argue, and he grew really weak after that. He had always been a little fragile. He suffered from a high blood pressure, and his heart was not that strong. He eventually slipped into depression and…then died."

I hadn't expected Jake to say that word, because I knew how hard it was to acknowledge a fact like that, but Jake had done it. I had been an orphan too. Even after all these years, I hadn't really been able to accept it. I didn't have any parents. I yearned for someone to call me, someone to give me surprises. I wanted to have someone I could call my own.

"I'm so sorry, Jake," I said, my voice breaking. Jake looked at me surprised, and then I began to talk. "I've spent years without my parents too. Throughout my childhood, I only wished for them to come back, to magically come alive again. But they never did. Even now, when I hear someone talk about their family, I feel jealous and yearn for a little portion of their happiness for myself. You must have had some good times with your Dad, right?" I asked.

"Of course, I did. He was a really good father and I miss him a lot, but I can't help blaming him," Jake said quietly.

"Blaming him for what?" I asked, although I had a feeling I already knew.

"After he died, the same thing happened all over again. My mom grew weak. She would call out to my dad and collapse sometimes, or faint. Her condition got from bad to worse. Soon after, I lost her too."

A tear slipped out of my eye. *Losing one parent was painful enough, but both?*

"I'm all alone too, you know," Jake concluded.

"And you're taking revenge by helping me expose the Wells?" I asked.

Jake stopped. "I knew you were smart, Rachel. I knew you had figured it out." He shook his head. "But I'm not helping you. I will get my own revenge." I had stopped too and I stared at him as his eyes flashed.

"Fine," I said as Jake walked on to catch up with me. "We'll expose the Wells…that's fine, really," I replied casually, "A piece of cake."

Jake laughed and I joined in too. We spotted a bench and sat on it to catch our breaths. "So," I began, "You've gotten used to being an orphan yet?"

Jake's face became serious. "Yeah, working hard for Bluebells has really taken my mind off things. It keeps me busy."

"How come you're still working at Bluebells?" I questioned.

"It's the only way I can see what Matthew is up to. Besides that, I know that he can't kick me out, because everyone likes me a lot and I've spotted and co-edited quite a few great books, including MOUT. He can't ditch me now," Jake explained.

"You've got it all planned out."

"You bet."

So do I, I thought.

"Thanks a lot for talking to me, Rachel. It's really nice to have someone I can talk to," Jake smiled and I grinned back.

Greed and ambition are different things

11

My 'fake-it-till-you-make-it' life soon resumed. Zara 'trained' me all over again, showing me how to walk, talk and laugh. She showed me what I had to wear at the event. She told me that she wanted me to do something really cool and extraordinary at the party.

"Breathe fire, maybe. It'll be just so wicked to see and your fans will love it..." Zara said.

I rolled my eyes. *What kind of an author breathes fire at her success party?*

"Don't you roll your eyes at me, Rachel Royce! You are-" Zara yelled.

"Yeah, I know, I'm totally whatever you're going to say," I replied to her angry face.

It was so much better hanging out with Sophia, Ashley and Jake.

"Darling, we're so, so proud of you!" Sophia said, as if I had won the Nobel Prize or something.

"Thanks, but it's not my novel. I'm just presenting it. If you want to be proud of someone, it should be Gwenyth," I replied, catching Jake's eye, who looked grave as ever, but smiled slightly at me.

"So modest-" Sophia chuckled. "Well, don't forget to review the last few bits of Torn. I'm going to visit my sister today, though I'll be back before your party. Jake edited the entire bit at the end and I feel so proud of him as well."

I was proud of Jake too. At least someone was happy. 'Someone' meaning Sophia, not Jake.

Ashley was really helpful. She gave me all these wonderful tips, in case I didn't know how to answer a question, or didn't want to reply to a fan.

Whenever Jake, Ashley and I got the time, we discussed how to bring Shaila there.

"Jake and I can simply slip away and get her. We'll ask her to meet us at Shalom Hills, the city, if she can, in order to save time," Ashley said.

"Good plan. I'll call Shaila and tell her that we'll be coming to fetch her," I replied.

"When will you call her?" Jake asked.

I scrunched my eyebrows, not having expected Jake to ask this question.

"Today, when I get home," I answered.

Jake nodded. "The sooner the better."

The rest of the day went by pretty fast and in a whirl of makeup.

As soon as I reached home that evening, I called Shaila up on the number she had given me.

I pressed the receiver to my ear and and my eyes grew wide in shock. For a second I thought I heard it wrong. No, it was just the automated voice saying, "This number does not exist."

~

"Obviously she doesn't have a phone number, otherwise we would have managed the entire editing process on call," Jake said, after I explained to him what happened.

"What are we going to do now?" Ashley squealed.

I spent the next few days really worried. *How in the world are we going to get Gwenyth—I mean, Shaila, from Shalom Hills?*

On top of that, Torn was growing more huge by the minute. Its posters were flashing all over the internet and had even started trending on social media sites with the hashtag #TornByTorn.

It was all very overwhelming. I had started to get really anxious, wondering what to do next.

When I came to work, I found Jake waiting for me.

"Jake! Nice to see you instead of Zara today," I smiled.

"Well, don't be so happy about it. I just wanted to tell you something, after which you're all Zara's," Jake replied, looking amused.

"So then, what's it that you want to tell me?" I asked.

"I wrote a letter to Shaila that day, telling her that I would come to pick her up the day after tomorrow, when the party is supposed to take place," Jake explained.

"What? How—what did she say?" I questioned.

"She said she would be ready and waiting," Jake smiled. "Shaila said she would meet us at Shalom Hills. Apparently, she asked her 'uncle' to take her there and he agreed. We'll get her, Rachel. Don't stress out."

It felt as if a huge load had been lifted off my shoulders.

"Oh God, Jake, I don't know what to say! Thank you so-"

"Don't rub it in, Rachel. Just don't ask me how I managed to talk to her – it was surreal."

"Whatever you say, Jake," I replied smiling.

"You need to meet Zara in her office. We'll talk later. Bye." Jake waved slightly and walked away.

I stared at his retreating figure. All those times he had yelled at me, his sudden bursts of anger, everything had been worth it, because the real Jake was so cool and nice. His mood swings used to bother me before, but I had started to get a hang of being with him.

I was feeling really light and happy as I walked towards Zara's office. I saw Ashley coming out of Zara's office, gently shutting the door behind her.

"Hey, Ashley!" I chirped.

Ashley looked really nervous when she saw me.

"Oh, hi Gw—Rachel!" She flashed an anxious smile.

"What's up?"

"Jake managed to contact Shaila. She'll come to Shalom Hills, and you guys can pick her up from there!" I explained.

"Really?" Ashley exclaimed, glancing back at the door of Zara's office. "That's great! Listen, I will talk later, right? Bye!" She left in a hurry.

I somehow handled Zara for the next two hours. She kept rambling on about hairstyles, makeup, celebrity guests, famous comedians, anchors, and what not. I tuned out most of what she was saying and imagined how fun it would be to watch both the Wells getting arrested by police officers and being driven away in those cars with deafening sirens. I realized that I had never actually seen Matthew Wells. I made a mental note to ask Jake about it later, but then I impulsively burst out, "Hey, Zara? What about your father? Will he be coming?"

I surprised Zara more than I had surprised myself. Her eyes became wide as she asked, "What?"

"You heard me," I replied coolly. I don't understand what had gotten into me that day. It must have been the excitement from hearing the news of Shaila's trip.

"Of course, my Dad will be there! He's the President of Bluebells, but I presume you already know that."

"Of course I do, Zara," I mimicked her tone. "Rumors just fly around here, don't they?"

"Yes, they do, Rachel. You must know that the best, mustn't you?" Zara snapped back.

I smirked at her annoyed face and walked out of her office. She didn't stop me.

It's going to be okay…I think.

-Ashley Wilson

12

The rest of the day passed quickly by. Jake, Ashley and I went over the final plan one last time.

"Ashley and I'll go to Shalom Hills by the same bus which you took. We'll meet Shaila there-"

"I know the directions to the ropeway, where we will pick up Shaila!" Ashley interrupted excitedly.

The old Jake would definitely have snapped at Ashley for having interrupted him. This Jake, however, just smiled.

"That's great, Ash. We'll have no trouble at all, then. We'll pick Shaila up and head right back here, where-" Jake trailed off, looking at Ashley.

"I'll hide Shaila in your office, and stay here with her," Ashley finished.

"Right. I'll give Rachel a heads-up on Shaila's status, and then we'll all head to the ground below," Jake explained.

"And when the time finally comes for me to talk, I'll take Shaila up with me and reveal everything," I conclude.

"What if someone asks about Shaila in the meantime?" Ashley questioned.

"Then Shaila's one of the makeup girls, or one of the party planners, or event manager—anything. Just make an excuse, alright? A convincing one," Jake answered.

"What'll we do once you reveal the truth to everyone?" Ashley asked.

Jake caught my eye. I knew I had to answer this question. "We'll improvise."

~

The day before the party passed by in a blur of rehearsals. Zara instructed me where to stand, what to do, etc. She told me about the popular news stations that were going to cover the event, and how to answer their questions.

Ashley instructed me on my makeup, hair and dress, and the entire schedule of the day. All this party planning would have been fun if it weren't for the guilt that was eating me up from inside.

When Ashley and Zara finally stopped pestering me, I went to my office and stared at the mirror again. The girl staring back at me looked tired and timid, slightly delicate, but her eyes were full of hope. If only Shaila got the recognition she deserved, perhaps the guilt would go away, I thought. I also realized that if the world supported Shaila, then I would become an instant villain in the story. I would be accused of identity theft and would get lawsuit after lawsuit slapped against me.

I was just praying like crazy for everything to work out alright, when Jake entered the room.

"Hi, Rachel." He sat on a chair. I realized that it was the same chair that he had kicked when we had argued. He saw it too and smiled at me.

"Don't worry, nothing will happen to it today," Jake said.

"I'm not worried about the chair. I'm more concerned about the plan," I replied.

"Everything will go just fine, Rachel. Chill out," Jake said, leaning back into the chair.

"Jake, I-"

"Don't. Nothing will go wrong, okay? You've got enough on your plate. Don't start thinking about this again. You're a wonderful person, Rachel. You could have kept your mouth shut and become a billionaire, but you chose the other way. You're going with your heart, and I really admire you for it, even though it isn't easy for you. You know what the consequences could be and how they might affect you, but you're not one to back down."

I didn't know how to respond to Jake's speech.

"You'll be fine, Rachel Royce," Jake patted the chair he was sitting on, as if patting me, "You'll do great."

It's complicated-so why even bother?

13

There I was, nervously sitting with a face pack on, just two hours before the party was to start. I couldn't believe how well they had fixed up the garden. It looked absolutely beautiful and glittery too. The food, prepared by the best chefs in town, was simply waiting there to be eaten and I could almost hear those appetizers calling out to me. But I knew better, because if I were to even look at them, Zara would start yelling at me.

Jake and Ashley had got Gwenyth there too, waiting without a glitch. He had told me this as soon as they got back, and I was itching to see her for myself, but Jake warned me against it, for someone could get suspicious. 'Someone' being Zara and her coworkers.

I sat there biting my lip, staring at my green face. My stylist had left me there, as Zara had beckoned her for an emergency. I felt bad for her; my stylist, not Zara.

Suddenly, the door burst open and both Sophia and my stylist rushed in and started speaking at the same time.

"Miss Ashley-makeup-sorry!" my stylist chattered on.

"I can't believe I forgot!" Sophia yelled.

I frantically looked from one to the other. I had no idea what they were blabbering about.

"Whoa, whoa!" I held my hands up and they stopped talking. "Sophia, you go first."

She was carrying a stack of important looking papers in her hand.

"Rachel—I'm sorry! It completely slipped from my mind, seriously-"

"What?!" I yelled.

"The manuscript!" she burst out. "You read the incomplete version; this is the final one that Jake finished editing three weeks ago!"

"Sophia, why-"

"Just start reading it right away!" She shoved the papers into my hands. "We have no time to lose! From Chapter 26 please," she continued, "Go, go and go!"

"I'll read it," I said calmly, but starting to feel a little anxious, surveying the bundle I had to read through.

"Quickly! I'll check on you later!" Sophia disappeared as suddenly as she had come.

"Miss, you can wash that now," my stylist said timidly.

"Yeah." I walked over to the sink and started splashing water over my face. "What was it that you were telling me before?"

"Miss Ashley was in Zara's office – she had the emergency. She still hadn't gotten dressed for the night, despite knowing that she has to go with Miss Zara to attend to the guests in less than an hour," she said as she started messing with my hair, yanking at it.

I waited for a moment, letting her words sink in and then frantically reached for my phone. "Miss!" my stylist warned, but I had already grabbed my phone. I typed a quick message to Jake, telling him to check on Shaila and then meet me ASAP.

I paused, wondering why Ashley had left Shaila alone, especially when she knew what a loony the author was. My head was stormed by the images of Shaila wandering around the building alone and bumping into Zara or Matthew Wells. I shuddered.

"Do you know where Matthew Wells is?" I asked my stylist.

"I think I saw him talking to Zara sometime before—he's already gone down, most probably," she replied.

I nodded and then turned my gaze to the manuscript and started reading as fast as my eyes could move. I realized that I had about 25 pages to read through - not as many as I had expected.

I read on and on, eyes widening and my mouth forming an 'o' of surprise. Involuntarily, my head drew closer to the book, but my stylist pulled me back by my hair, trying to straighten them with a rod. My hair felt hot against my skin, but I was pretty sure that my face had gone pale from what I was reading.

I took my time, reading and re-reading, but my brain was simply refusing to acknowledge what I learnt. By the time I finished, my stylist had left and another girl had come in for makeup.

I closed my eyes, feeling her brush move across my face. All that was going on in my mind was just the one sentence, "How could this be possible?!" Over and over again, a desperate question.

A knock on the door just then made me jump.

"Don't open your eyes, the eyeliner is still wet."

I sat there with my eyes closed, as I heard her open the door, and a familiar voice asked, "Rachel?"

"Jake!" I yelled and it took all my willpower to not open my eyes. The girl resumed applying makeup again, and I sensed Jake taking a seat next to me.

"Shaila's fine, Rachel. She, um, I-" he hesitated, unsure perhaps of the makeup girl.

The girl realized what was happening and quickly finished adding the last touches to my makeup.

"Just change your shoes and wear this bracelet. That's all," she announced and left hastily. I opened my eyes and saw Jake smiling at me.

"Jake, what—who wrote this manuscript?" I half-yelled.

"Well, Shaila did it, of course," he said, looking slightly flustered.

"But it—that's not possible!" I replied.

Jake gives me a steady look and it made me even more jumpy.

"Didn't you read it? It says Jane wrote the book and got it published, but the credit went to someone else! Exactly-like-it-happened to Shaila!" I screamed.

New situations call for old tricks

14

Jake was still in his silent mode, which made me want to punch him in the face. *Why doesn't he say or do something? I need an explanation for this.*

"What do you think, did Shaila predict the future?" Jake asked as I stared at him, open-mouthed. "Jake, don't you think you should've told me about this? About-"

"And how would that have helped you?" Jake asked, evidently irritated, and his annoyance annoyed me even more. He walked out of the room, and I had no choice but to follow him.

"What about the manuscript?" I asked angrily. "It just isn't possible, it's completely-"

Jake didn't even bother to look at me. "It's just a coincidence, Rachel. Don't you have other things to worry about right now?"

I realized that Jake didn't want to talk about it at that moment, but I was defiant. "Don't tell me you just forgot to tell me about it, Jake. You knew perfectly well that I hadn't read it. Why were you so keen on preventing me from reading the manuscript?"

My confrontation alarmed Jake. He looked unsure of what to say.

"This is exactly why I didn't want you reading it. I knew you would get all hyper and get distracted. I'll explain it to you later, I promise. Right now, we have to check on Shaila."

"You preferred me not reading the ending over me getting seriously distracted?" I questioned. "What if the reporters asked me something about the ending? It would have been game over for everyone!"

"I made a mistake," Jake snapped. "Happy? Excuse me, but I really need to find the true writer of MOUT. Sorry, if I don't have the time to answer your silly doubts for once."

He walked away, taking long strides. I ran over to him, trying to keep up.

"Where's Shaila?" I asked, still furious.

"She's in my office and she's fine. I kind of locked her in there."

"You did what?!"

"Don't ask," Jake said and I felt like I was about to break out in a torrent of abusive words, when he turned left and told me, "I'll pick Shaila up. You go downstairs. We'll meet there."

He looked at me, tired. "I'm sorry, okay?" he said and then turned to leave without a second glance.

I marched to the ground, and my anger instantly got replaced by anxiety. All I could see was just one side of the stage. The other side, no doubt, had been occupied by reporters, famous celebrities, and critics, all of whom were waiting for me to arrive.

I stared down at what I was wearing. It was a sequinned and glittery silver coloured gown that looked quite chic, but hey! I was supposed to be a writer, not a freaking pop star. I rolled my eyes at Zara's idiocy.

I went backstage and saw people running in every direction; people with clipboards, people with suits and dresses, even waiters carrying plates of food.

My hunger vanished as soon as I spotted Zara coming towards me, accompanied by a middle aged man, who was wearing a silk tie, and a scowl on his face.

"Rachel, where have you been?" Zara asked.

"I've got a show to run here!" Matthew Wells yelled at me.

"Pleased to meet you too, Mr. Wells," I said, smiling sweetly. "You better not talk to me like that in front of your reporters. It could lead to a lot of bad publicity."

"Save the sarcasm for another occasion, Royce," he glared at me.

"Guess what, Mr. Wells? It might be you who calls the shots, but I am the one who runs the show. So unless you want me to talk junk about Bluebells, don't you dare mess with *me*," I retorted, all my anger coming back. "I'll meet you on stage," I said to the Wells and was about to go on stage when I spotted Jake tugging Shaila along with him.

"Jake!" I called out, relieved to see both of them in one piece.

"Rachel!" Shaila squealed and rushed towards me. "I've missed you so much I thought-"

Ashley joined our trio just then.

"So, are you going on stage with Shaila?" she asked me, and I suddenly remembered the fact that she had left Shaila alone to meet Zara. However, I decided to leave the matter for then, since everything had worked out fine up till that point.

"First, I'll go on stage and welcome everyone, then I'll call Shaila onstage and reveal the truth. Fine?" I turned my gaze from Ashley to Jake. Both looked slightly nervous; Ashley kept glancing over my shoulder and Jake nodded uncertainly.

"Jake, you will help Shaila come onstage, alright? While Ashley can keep an eye out for Zara and Matthew Wells. I'm pretty sure they'll be in the crowd, but-"

"We got it, Rachel," Ashley interrupted.

I blinked nervously. "Okay, then," I took a deep breath, "Let's do this thing!"

I step out onto the stage, heart pounding, and almost got blinded by all the lights focussed on me.

Every single news crew had switched on its own light and the familiar 'click' noise of the camera fit right in with the chaos in my head.

The celebs, critics and everyone else present there applauded my arrival onstage. The anchor, who had been telling a joke, stopped abruptly in the middle, not bothering to say the punch line anymore.

"And there she is, ladies and gentlemen! The writer of the most phenomenal trilogy on the planet! Gwenyth Parlow!"

I blinked and smiled, blinded by all those lights. I almost corrected the anchor, to say that my name is Rachel, but stopped just in time.

"No!" I heard someone shout behind me, and I turned in reflex. When I saw nothing, I turned quickly to face the audience again, my mind racing.

Who said that? Who yelled that? Shaila? I still couldn't fathom how in the world her story's ending matched her real life so precisely. It was far too twisted to be a simple coincidence. *Perhaps she had a premonition.*

I got lost thinking about the various possible scenarios, when I suddenly realized that I was onstage, in front of the entire world. It was definitely not a good time to start daydreaming.

My mind reeled. I held my hands up to quieten everybody down and said, "MOUT has inspired millions of readers all over the planet. It's a record breaking series and I'm amazed at how the world has reacted to the trilogy. Today, I would like you all to meet the-" I took a deep breath, as I felt my palms getting sweaty- "The real genius behind the books."

I turned around to look back at the stage, but the lights were so bright, even on the stage, that I couldn't see anything.

"Ladies and gentlemen, meet the real Gwenyth Parlow – Shaila Faye." I prayed to the Gods for Jake to have heard me.

I bravely looked at the crowd which was staring at me, confused by my announcement. Everyone waited with bated breaths for someone to come out, for something to happen. But nothing did. I looked back again, but there was no one there.

"Rachel!" I heard someone screaming. I looked to the stage's left, where I had heard my name being called from. I squinted and saw Shaila flailing her arms about and yelling, while two burly men gripped her by her arms. I looked at the crowd and saw Zara and Matthew Wells shouting at me.

I grabbed my sequinned dress, took a running start and jumped right off the stage.

The times don't change - people do

15

I planned my fall correctly and managed to land smoothly on my feet. I think my gown tore slightly at the hem, and I caught a glimpse of my black crocs. I had been in such a hurry that I forgot to wear the sparkly heels that Ashley had set aside for me.

I cannot be thinking about that right now. The crowd is gasping and all the cameras are aimed at me, clicking pictures furiously. After all, it's not everyday that the best writer of the world jumps off the stage, right?

I could barely see anything amidst the blinding lights. I put out a hand to block them and yelled, "Shaila!"

I couldn't see her anywhere. It was as if she, along with her assaulters, had just disappeared. "Shaila!" I screamed again, as I went on thinking, "This cannot be happening."

I felt like a complete fool. I had just jumped off stage to save a girl who wasn't even here. My hairstyle had gotten all messed because of the leap I took, and I just stood there, confused, as the entire world (not really true) watched me, baffled.

Everyone was wondering what to do when a loud 'screeeee' sound from the mike caused everyone to snap their attention to the front. The camera men resumed taking pictures of the stage, and I was left there, forgotten in complete darkness.

"I'm going to keep it nice and simple," the voice said, but I couldn't place it. The electronic flair of a mike completely changes the voice of the person talking into it. To add to my frustration, I couldn't even see the person on stage. All I could see was the base of the stage, since the lights behind the stage were shining back intensely.

"There is no Gwenyth Parlow. There is no Shaila Faye. The real writer of MOUT is-"

The speaker paused, and the world held its breath for a long moment.

"Me."

~

Everything broke into a frenzy. Half of the media got busy snapping pictures of the speaker, while the other half went after me.

I struggled to get past the reporters and the cameramen. People kept asking me, "Why did you do it?" and "Your game is up. What are your plans now?" and other confusing things.

I got lost amidst a sea of media men. People bumped into each other and into me, trying to hear what I had to say. I didn't have anything to tell the world at that moment. I just needed to get away from everyone.

I pushed, struggled, and even hit one of the reporters, pushing his mike away from my face. Everyone backed off after that. I took advantage of the situation and walk away.

I grabbed my dress and ran forward towards the stage, where the other half of the crowd was still taking pictures incessantly.

This time, I went around the entire crowd. All I wanted was just a glimpse of the speaker, who had claimed to be the writer of MOUT.

I was carefully making my way around the crowd when I saw two policemen escorting Zara and Matthew out.

Both of them were in handcuffs. A third policeman made his way towards me.

"No! Please! Just- just let me see who's on stage, I'll-" I started.

"Don't you recognize who it is?" Zara screamed viciously.

I turned my head towards the stage, while the policemen grabbed me.

I looked at the speaker and our eyes met for a confused moment.

All I could do was to shake my head and whisper, "Jake?"

Life is cruel - or are we?

16

A police station would probably be a boring place for one who doesn't have much to think about.

Matthew and Zara Wells were immediately convicted and charged for numerous crimes like theft, taking money illegally out of a private bank account etc, etc. They had a huge lawsuit charge slapped on them as well, and their schemes finally came to an end.

The police was actually confused about what to do with me. I didn't really know whether what I had been doing was illegal (I had guessed it, but that's another matter). I had simply followed the terms of a contract which stated that the author didn't have a problem with me acting as her face for the public. *They should let me go,* I thought.

But the real problem was that even I had broken the terms of that contract. That could result in a lawsuit from the writer, and a fine/three months' stay. *Oh boy!*

That is, if the writer wished to press charges against me.

If.

I sat there, waiting. The policemen debated whether I should get charged for identify theft as well. I didn't bother to listen to their argument. I was too busy with my own mental debates.

The reporters had crowded outside the police station, some pressing their faces and lenses against the glass of the window, others trying to persuade the guard to let them in.

Every request, of course, was rejected.

Suddenly, there was a huge commotion outside and all the media reporters turned away from the windows. Two policemen opened the door to help a visitor inside and he stepped in, looking visibly shaken.

Jake.

I stared at him and he glanced at me, then his eyes slide away from mine. He went to sit in a chair with his back towards me.

I resisted the urge to yell at him and sat there, patiently. Jake discussed his options with the police officers. They started things off with the Wells'.

"Yes, yes," he said, "I want them punished for every single charge you can think of." His statement made things go a lot faster and they soon turned their focus to me.

"You could file a lawsuit for identity theft, or go to court for a sentence or a fine," one of the policemen suggested. Jake flipped through papers, thinking hard. He did that for a long time, which was fine by me, because I needed some planning time as well.

"No charges will be pressed against her," Jake finally said. "I do, however, want my money back, which amounts to-"

"It's a hefty sum, but sir, you can take her penthouse. That should cover most of it, leaving-" He punched some numbers in a calculator and said, "$15,000."

"I'd like that money back in instalments," Jake replied. "I won't be filing any complaints against her, but if I don't get my money back, I will. You can tell her that." He stood up to leave.

"Why, Jake, are you so afraid to say it to me yourself?" I asked. Jake whirled around, went red on seeing me and turned back to face the front again.

"Oh? So you can't even look at me now?" I yelled, trembling. "You can't face me, can you? You've always-"

"What do you want, Rachel?" he finally asked, sneering.

I folded my arms. "You certainly know what you want, don't you?"

"Yes! I want my money back!" Jake screamed. "I want my hard-earned money back! The money you spent like it was worthless!"

"Didn't you think even once that you could've told me all about this?" I asked, being on the verge of tears. "What about all those good times we shared? The times when you were with me? What happened to them, Jake?" I yelled back, standing up. "And this is how you repay me? This-"

"Me? You've got to figure out who's repaying who, Rachel. I saved you from a lawsuit, a fine-"

"Why did you, Jake? Why? Go ahead, file a case! Do it!" I shrieked. "You can't, can you? Because you know I've already suffered a lot for you and your books. You know I've helped you and you accept it. Yet, you're greedy enough to demand 15,000 bucks from me! The guilt will eat you up one day, Jake." I calmed down a bit and said, "It will bother you every minute of the day till you lose your mind." I cocked my head to one side. "What happened with me will happen to you, Jake," I paused, "And this time, no one will be there to help you." Angry tears started to stream down my face. "No one."

Jake gave me a scathing look and walked out, without bothering to look back.

~

I watched Jake's retreating figure and as he opened the door to leave, the cameramen got on their toes after him. Some of them got a glimpse of me as well, I make sure that they did.

The door slammed shut behind him. I took a deep breath, wiped the tears off my face and sat down in the same chair that Jake had been sitting on. I flicked back my hair and looked at the policeman, slightly smiling, and asked him, "What's next?"

Not all who are lost, wander

17

5 YEARS LATER…

I woke up minutes before my alarm was to go off. I slid into my shoes and went up to the window, gazing out at the beautiful scenery in front of me. I stood there, looking at the children going to school. They were laughing at and poking each other. I smiled at their childish ways, simultaneously feeling that I had forgotten to do something.

TRRING!!!

I jumped. Of course.

I shut the alarm clock and glanced at the old newspaper clipping pasted on my wall. My breath got caught in my throat yet again as I stared at the headline.

"The Truth About MOUT is Out!"

It was a huge article about the entire scandal, but I didn't bother reading it again. I knew more than what the world knew, but even that was not the entire truth. Only one person knew that, but he hadn't bothered to tell anyone.

Maybe.

I was over the MOUT Episode. The policemen had made me sign some paperwork that day, and then gave me a ticket to a place far away, as I had requested. I stepped out onto my balcony. It was a pretty morning, with birds flying and sunlight peeking out from behind the clouds. The trolley cars on the ropeway were still; the service didn't start until…I don't know. Why would I have bothered anyway?

I loved Shalom Hills.

~

I was sitting in my living room, fully dressed, because Cindy (my neighbor) had told me that someone was coming to meet me, and she had sounded quite excited. She was in her early twenties, and it was unusual for her to act so jumpy over a visitor. Whoever was coming must be really special, I thought.

I mentally made a list of all the potential visitors, smiling at the memory of some of them. My best guess was the electrician's visit, so I could finally install a TV in my house, as Cindy had been begging me to do for the last two years. I wondered whether it was laundry day that day or not, when the door bell rang. I opened the door, expecting to see the electrician on the other side with his tool box and bad breath. Instead, I found Cindy standing there, grinning from ear to ear.

"You are going to get so surprised, Rachel!" She pulled a mock hurt face. "I wish you'd told me before."

"Told you-" I started to ask but my voice trailed off as Cindy moved aside to reveal the person standing behind her. I wondered how I could ever have missed seeing him.

I stared at the dark eyes, the light brown hair, the grim set of his jaw, which always made it look like he was about to cry. He stared back at me, and I realized how much we both had changed since we had last seen each other.

"Rachel," he said, softly and painfully.

"Jake."

~

I used to curse Jake every day since the police station incident.

Why hadn't he told me that he was the author of the MOUT? Did he ever even see me as a friend? Did I ever see him as a friend? The questions were endless.

I had also walked away, like Jake had done, but on a different path. While he took the road to fame and fortune, I went ahead on the path that was the furthest from his path.

I went away from the world of fame, glam, and media. I disappeared for the world; the world disappeared for me.

Occasionally, Cindy brought me newspapers or magazines which tried to explain what exactly happened to me. No one had guessed it correctly; even if they would have, they couldn't know it for sure.

Jake had betrayed me. Perhaps not betrayed, because that's a really powerful word, but he did lie and hide a lot of things from me. I did too, but that was different – *or was it?* I really could never be sure.

Since this whole MOUT thing was enough to make me go crazy, I realized one day the most simple solution to my problem.

Stop thinking.

It wasn't easy, of course, but I did, and found peace and calm in the secluded retreats of Shalom Hills.

But a part of me still remained desperate to talk to Jake, yell at him, scream and break things; the part of me that wanted just one question answered.

Why?

~

"Well, see ya later, Rachel, and you too Mr. Parker!" Cindy waved us goodbye and walked away towards her own house. Jake stood there in the doorway, tapping his foot and scratching his hair nervously. I caught myself biting my lip.

"Come in," I found myself saying and led him to the couch. We sat facing each other, a table between us.

I looked at him, expecting him to say something, and realized that he was waiting for me to do the same. We both looked away, not knowing what to say.

Awkward.

Jake cleared his throat and tugged at his coat in a self-conscious manner. I noticed that he was wearing several precious gems on his fingers.

He saw me observing the rings and quickly stuffed his hands inside his pockets. I coughed nervously.

"You were right, Rachel," he said finally and I jumped on hearing his voice after all these years. I waited for him to go on.

"I can't handle the guilt. You were always so nice to me and I treated you like dirt. Not charging you with a lawsuit wasn't even the least I could have done for you. I made you return the $15,000 you had received for simply doing your work. That was just me being a jerk."

I had paid that off last year. Luckily, I had been depositing $1000 every month, so I didn't have to burn a hole in my pocket. Still, I had managed to return his money.

"I'm sorry, Rachel," Jake added, taking a deep breath. "I've been looking for you for almost a year now. The policemen at the station refused to tell me where you had gone."

I had specifically requested them to keep all my details private as I didn't want anyone to come after me, especially him. But more than Jake, I didn't want any reporters to find me.

I nodded, egging Jake on to continue.

"What do you want to know, Rachel? I know I left abruptly without any explanation at all. You must have a lot of questions."

I did have a lot of questions. I thought carefully and decided to ask everything from the start.

"Why did my training take place at Hilton offices instead of Bluebells?" I finally asked, and a smile appeared on Jake's face on hearing my voice. A sad one.

"The Wells were afraid of me. I knew lots of people at Bluebells who had been friends with my father. They thought that I might take help from the people at Bluebells to expose them."

"Then why did they include you in the secret at all?"

Jake shrugged. "They probably thought that I would find out one way or another anyway. It was better for them to have me on their side. The Wells also felt that it was a good way to make me think that they were nice, but I knew their real intentions."

"So they just told you that they were planning to betray Gwenyth—you, without thinking of the consequences? I'm confused."

Jake shook his head and made a face. "They had me under watch the entire time. That's why Ashley had been instructed to gain my trust. Same goes for you."

It had all started to make sense now.

"So when Shaila was taken away by the guards that night, that-"

"Was all because of Ashley. She had been Zara's secret spy all that time, following us around. All that sweet talk, that friendship was nothing but clever planning."

"And you had no idea of it?" I asked surprised.

Jack shifted uneasily. "Of course, I did. In fact, that is one of the reasons why I decided to let Ashley come with us. I knew that she would report her findings to Zara, while letting me do whatever I wanted. Otherwise, how would I have come on stage on the night of the party if you had told everyone that Shaila was the writer of MOUT? You had been so determined to follow the plan."

"But…I did tell everyone, Jake."

He smiled softly and said, "But Shaila didn't say a word about being the writer. In fact, she didn't come on stage at all."

I gasped. "So you meant it to happen that way! You knew that Ashley would tell Zara what we had been doing, so her men would grab Shaila before she could get on stage! You also knew that I wouldn't have let anything happen to Shaila and would run after her, so you could take the stage and tell the world that you are the real writer!"

"Yes," Jake said. "That's exactly what my plan was. I also knew that you wouldn't help me unless you met Shaila, so I had to hire this actress - actresses, in fact – to go along with your plan."

"But how come you didn't let me meet that old lady? The one you described –two front teeth missing – wild hair?" I asked.

"She couldn't speak what I wanted her to," Jake explained, "She refused to wear the Bluetooth device-"

"Excuse me?"

"Shaila's hearing aid was actually a Bluetooth earpiece. I had been telling her what to say the entire time. One of the buttons on her dress had a concealed recorder, so I could hear all that you said."

"Ohhh," was all that I could manage to say.

"Yeah, the old woman wasn't nearly as comfortable with the modern technology as the other actress who played Shaila. The old one's accent was weird too – so I hired the younger one."

"Wow," I said. Jake looked at me curiously, visibly taken aback by my comment. "I mean, you must have done a lot of planning for all this."

"Indeed, I did." Jake replied simply and I nodded. We sat in silence for a few moments before I asked, "How, and why, did you choose me for the job?"

"Zara wanted you badly when she found out that you are an orphan. You know, you had no close relatives, no contacts, so you were unlikely to tell anyone about this secret and were easy to keep an eye on too. Sophia did some research on you and found out that you had won several awards in oration and debating during your school days as well. We found out that you had been looking to be a spokesman of some sort - so we felt that you were the perfect candidate."

In the five years that I didn't see Jake, I sometimes imagined that I had been chosen for a reason that had something to do with my parents. Hoped, even. However, life doesn't work that way. It takes all your wishes and fears, analyses them, and throws your hurdles back at you based on that. Sometimes, you get what you want and at other times, you don't.

Mostly, it's the manner in which you get/don't get your way, that matters more than anything else.

"The contract," I said suddenly, "It had another language on it besides English."

"That was German," Jake answered.

I was about to ask him why such a contract had German on it, when Jake started to explain by himself.

"Through the letters I had sent, I told everyone that I wanted my contract to be written both in English and in German, which was supposed to be my native language."

"And they agreed to that?" I asked.

"Well, yes. They did have to let this one thing go the author's way, since they were robbing 'her' of so much money anyway."

"But why did you do it?" I questioned.

"The contract you signed, Rachel, mentioned in English that the author had absolutely no problem with you appearing as her public image. However, the part in German stated that no notice was to be taken of the part written in English. I felt it would be convenient to fool you."

I gaped at Jake. "That way, if anything had gone wrong, the Wells could have shown the contract and trapped you," Jake finished. "It was a fake contract."

"Oh my God." I didn't know what else to say. This was extreme. I had never imagined the situation to have been this complicated.

"Jake, does that mean that you were both the writer and the editor of the book?"

"Yes, Rachel. In fact, I actually felt glad when I wasn't offered to edit MOUT. It was better for me to co-edit the series, since I really did want it to be the best. Torn, however, was my book alone. I didn't let Sophia read any draft except for the final one, because I knew it was perfect as it was."

I raised my eyebrows at Jake's words. "You're so modest, Jake!"

Jake laughed. "Yes, call it arrogance, but seriously, Rachel, do you think it deserved any changes?"

"No," I found myself saying.

"Sophia agreed with me too, so did the whole world. Besides," Jake sat up straight, "Too many cooks spoil the broth."

"Yeah," I said, "But just one cook can't do much good to it either."

Stupid mistakes
Wise learnings unhappy endings

18

I put on some water to boil for tea. Jake followed me into the kitchen and leaned against the counter.

"I'm surprised you haven't asked anything about the ending of Torn yet," he said, stuffing his hands into the pockets of his pants, gazing at me.

"I was about to," I replied, adding two spoons of sugar. "Tell me."

"There were two reasons. Firstly, I thought that by not letting you read the ending, you wouldn't be able to answer questions about the novel correctly. That way, even if you decided to back out of the original plan, you would still get caught easily."

"But Sophia didn't know this," I replied.

"Yes. My backup plan failed. But you acted exactly the way I had wanted you to, so my original plan remained intact."

I bit my nail and pushed my hair back, thinking.

"I also wanted to add that last bit as an ode to you," Jake explained timidly.

Completely taken by surprise, I nearly dropped the tea strainer. "What?" I asked, unbelievingly.

"You inspired me, Rachel. You made me want to get even with the Wells, and I admired you. You lived with the guilt, but you managed somehow to pull through every press conference, and-" he stopped, "MOUT became successful because of you too. You acted perfectly, Rachel, and I can't help but think sometimes that I gained many fans because of you."

I strained the tea and handed a cup to Jake. I took a sip from my own cup, waiting for him to continue.

"I felt angry whenever you attended an interview or something. I had done all the hard work, but you were the one reaping all the rewards. But today, Rachel, I'm so thankful to you. I–just-" he sighed, biting his lips. "Thank you so much."

I tried to smile, but it came out lopsided. I controlled my emotions and looked at Jake.

"I wanted Sam to be the writer, but it just couldn't work out. I know he was your favorite character-"

"Is," I interrupted.

"What?"

"Is my favourite character." I tilted my head to one side, smiling slightly.

Jake grinned. "Yeah, but it couldn't work out with him, so I had to give it to Jane. It matched the script nicely, don't you think?"

"It did. But when I read it, I thought-"

"That Shaila had…I don't know, an intuition that the same thing was happening to her too?" Jake asked.

"It seemed that way, yes," I answered matter-of-factly.

"I also did it that way so MOUT would gain a lot of publicity, more than it was already gaining," Jake said. He couldn't meet my eye.

"So what happened to MOUT then?" I asked.

"You don't know?" Jake asked.

"I've cut myself off from the world, Jake. Shalom Hills, remember?"

"Oh, right." He cleared his throat and continued, "After the big reveal that night, I was bombarded with questions about why I hadn't said anything before, why I pressed charges against the Wells and none against you, why I did what I did; the whole lot." He paused. "I answered all the questions, not exactly telling lies, but…um, fabricating the truth, you could say. I didn't answer any questions related to you. Whenever it came to you, I just told them to find you and ask you all the questions they wanted. I got what I wanted, Rachel."

"And what is that?"

"For MOUT to become the greatest thing on this planet. And it did. But it did not happen in the way

I had imagined exactly. Unfortunately, the scandal became bigger than the trilogy itself."

"Didn't you expect that to happen?" I questioned.

"Partly yes, but to this extent…no, never," Jake answered.

"What happened to Ashley, Sophia, the Wells?"

"I'll start with the most obnoxious first," Jake said. "The Wells, Zara and Matthew, were charged with so many offences that they could never get out of the trap I had set up for them. They filed for bankruptcy three years ago. They lost some cases against me and Matthew was sentenced with a year, while Zara got 6 months."

"Oh my God. What for?"

"Making money by illegal means, not paying taxes, forging contracts - you name it, they did it."

"Where are they now?"

"I have no idea. They simply disappeared. I'm going to find them once I get back to the city from Shalom Hills."

"Don't, Jake," I heard myself say. "It'll be of no use."

"I just want to make sure they aren't tormenting another person like they did with us. I want to make sure that their chapter is truly closed."

I took a deep sigh, shaking my head slightly. "What about Ashley?"

"She fled the scene soon after the Wells got arrested. I checked on her a few months back - she's working as a sales clerk at a brand store."

"No charges against her?"

Jake shrugged. "She didn't do anything wrong, technically. That was Zara's department. I let her go. I didn't want her, Ashley, ruining her life because of a stupid mistake."

Stupid mistakes. I wished I could also have done something about those.

"Sophia?" I asked.

"Nothing happened to her, either. All she did was edit some books. She edited MOUT, Rachel. I still talk with her sometimes, and she is the editor–in-chief at one of the biggest publishing companies in New York now. I did tell her one thing, though."

I looked at him curiously.

"To never, ever tell anyone that I had co-edited the books as her assistant," Jake replied to my look.

"Of course," I said.

"What do you mean?"

"You had it all planned, didn't you, Jake? That's-that's great," I replied, tripping over my words.

"Are you angry at me, Rachel?" Jake set his tea cup down. "I'm sorry. I wasn't completely honest with you, but I did my best to make amends, don't you think so?"

"You did, Jake...it's not that." I grew close to tears and I bit my lip so hard that I could taste blood.

"Then what is it, Rachel? You're clearly upset about something." Jake looked very concerned, and I felt like an absolute traitor.

"You don't get it, do you, Jake?" I asked. "You used me-"

"I'm sorry, Rachel. I shouldn't have done that. I was greedy, selfish—what not. But I want to fix things now. Come on-"

"Yes, you used me, Jake. But-"

"I used you, yes, but Rachel, I feel truly sorry for having played those games-"

"SHUT UP!" I burst out. "Stop it! Let me speak!"

Jake got surprised by my outburst, but kept quiet all the same.

"You used me, Jake...but more than that, I was the one who used you," I finally spoke.

Is deception better? Or brutal truth?

19

It was true.

If Jake had it all planned out already, then so had I. I had always been one step ahead of him. Every single move I had made, had an intention behind it. And it all played to my advantage.

"What?" Jake asked, evidently confused.

I placed my own cup in the sink and went back to the living room, to take a seat on a couch. I expected Jake to follow me, but he lingered in the doorway of the kitchen, his face all scrunched up.

"You were planning your revenge with Zara and I was helping you, Jake. You assumed that you and Zara were the opposing battling sides, while I was just a pawn, right? A step to be taken on the ladder of success?" I asked.

"Yeah, I guess," Jake answered, baffled. "But what-"

"Jake," I said, squeezing my sweaty palms over the couch cover. "When I first signed the contract, I admit, I was ignorant. I had no idea that it would become the worst decision of my life. But I had to fix it when I realized what I had gotten myself into. I first considered partnering up with Zara, but it obviously wouldn't have worked out. I had to team up with someone who was trustworthy, reliable and smart."

"And you chose me," Jake finished.

"Yes. When I went with Ashley to Shalom Hills, I found myself second-guessing about the whole team thing. I thought that Ashley and I would be great too. But then she told me your story, Jake, and I knew that I had made the right choice." I picked up a pillow and placed it on my lap, while twiddling with its corners. "My original plan had been to team up with you so that I could meet Gwenyth somehow. After that, I had planned to convince Gwenyth and make her feel sorry for me, so that-"

"When you reveal the truth to the whole world, Gwenyth would be there to protect you, since she'd be grateful to you," Jake completed my sentence, his eyebrows drawn closer, trying to comprehend.

"Correct. But after we met Shaila, I realized that I couldn't completely depend on her to get me out of that mess. She was so eccentric, so I decided to continue the partnership that I had established with you."

"So that when the truth were to come out, I would help you, even if Shaila didn't!" Jake exclaimed, his face pale.

I looked at him, pursing my lips and blinking twice, in an attempt to hold back my tears. "As you already know, my plan worked. It worked too well."

Jake rested his arm against the frame of the door, supporting his body weight on it. He shook his head, not knowing what to say.

"You thought that I was the pawn, while the real battle had been between you and Zara," I said, shaking my head. "It was always my game, Jake. You were the pawn. We beat Zara. I won."

Jake looked aghast. He stared at me, his eyes visibly angry and hurt.

"You used me? You used *me,* Rachel? After all the help and support I gave you?" He stomped his foot and yelled, "I can't believe it!"

Jake's anger annoyed me. "Yeah, so maybe I did use you, Jake, but you're not so innocent yourself. All those lies you told me, the wild goose chase you sent me on…I could go on forever. Your original plan was indeed to trap me along with Zara and Matthew. I used you to save my own skin. But you, Jake, used me for revenge."

"That's why I came here! To apologize to you for having done all this! I had never imagined, however, that you had had your own plans," Jake said viciously.

I squared my shoulders, calming myself down.

"Now we're even, Jake. We lied to each other for our own selfish purposes and we both got what we wanted. I'm sorry if what I did upset you. I accept your apology."

Jake raked his hand through his hair, exasperated.

"Well, don't expect me to do the same," he said and walked out, slamming the door behind him.

Pain is inevitable, Suffering is optional

20

I sipped my tea cautiously, staring at the computer screen. The day's newspaper was lying to my side, momentarily forgotten. It's time was yet to come, as at that moment, there were more important things that required my attention.

It had been a week since Jake visited me. For a few days after his visit, I couldn't eat, sleep, or think properly. My mind kept wandering back to him and what he had said. I felt the guilt clawing at me from the inside. But soon after, when the pain slowly subsided, I realized some crucial things.

Jake and I had both lied to one another. We had lied to the world, concealed our true identities and put on a mask for the show. When all of it ended and the truth came out, we found ourselves shocked to see each other's true faces.

The fact that Jake had lied to me didn't hurt the most, but that Jake didn't consider me good enough to confide in me the truth of his identity was the most painful thing to accept. He hadn't trusted me enough to tell me that he was the real author of MOUT. He had been my only friend.

Though, when his dark secrets were revealed, it saddened me deeply.

Jake had undergone exactly the same thing. He was shocked to know that I had used him, and I couldn't blame him for that. The same thing had happened with me too. With time, I eventually forgave him.

I decided to put the entire MOUT episode behind me. I knew that I had made mistakes in the past, but I couldn't let them control my future. I knew I deserved better than that. I had to let go.

I had made progress forgiving Jake, and then by asking for *his* forgiveness in return. The fact that he didn't, bothered me. I had come to realize that it was much easier to say sorry for your mistakes than to forgive someone else for theirs. I hoped for Jake to realize this too one day. Perhaps then he would forgive me.

Or perhaps he wouldn't.

I was shrugging off my past. It was not easy, but I had faith in myself. Still, there were some things about my past that I couldn't help but want to know. For me, it was my parents. I wanted to know if they really loved me as much I had always imagined them to. I *needed* to know it. I couldn't hear this from them, of course, but a distant relative was the next best thing.

I contacted the orphanage via e-mail and they gave me a phone number in return. My heartbeat quickened as I read it over and over again. A popup window suddenly appeared on my screen, asking me if I wanted to purchase a copy of *Torn*. I shook my head and closed it without a second glance.

I picked up my phone and dialed the number with trembling fingers. It's funny how a phone call can change the future in unimaginable ways, both good or bad. I knew the difference very well. I hoped this one to be the best of all.

Someone picked up on the third ring at the other end. I took a deep breath and said, "Hello?"

About the Author

Saloni Hazela is 15 years old, and a student of class 10 at DPS Gurgaon. She is meritorious in her academics. Her hobbies include reading and horse riding. She avidly participates in debates, as well as the cultural and social activities at school. This is her first book, of many to come.